CU00894670

Put a Saddle on the Pig

Also by Sam McBratney
available from Methuen Children's Books
and Mammoth

Funny How the Magic Starts

available from Mammoth for younger readers

Jimmy Zest

The Jimmy Zest All-Stars

Zesty

SAM McBRATNEY

Put a Saddle on the Pig

BUCKS COUNTY LIBRARY

S
94

MBC 216138

METHUEN

First published in Great Britain 1992
by Methuen Children's Books,
a division of Reed International Books Ltd
Michelin House, 81 Fulham Road, London SW3 6RB.
Text copyright © 1992 Sam McBratney
Printed in Great Britain by Butler and Tanner Limited,
Frome and London

A CIP catalogue record for this title is available from
the British Library.

The right of Sam McBratney to be identified as the author of this
work has been asserted by him in accordance with the Copyright
Designs and Patent Act, 1988

ISBN 0 416 19032 4

One

There are times when mothers can be strange and impulsive creatures. Why should Mrs Victoria Clement suddenly decide to up and move house after nearly nineteen years of living in Ashfield Manor Mews without a word of complaint? Her daughter Laura was appalled by the whole idea.

'What has got into you, Mummy?' she said. 'We like it here, you're always telling people how it's handy to everywhere and I don't see why we should move.'

They were working together in the small garden at the front of the house. Mrs Clement dug up a clump of bulbs and appeared to examine them for rot. The disgusting mass in her mother's hand made Laura think of onions gone wrong, but of course they couldn't be onions, not here where Mother liked a 'show'.

'I thought that young people nowadays were supposed to welcome change,' her

5

mother said carelessly.

'Small changes, yes. Big changes – no. They can plunge your whole life into darkness, uncertainty and despair.'

'Really.'

'Yes, really.'

They both smiled, but in truth the conversation had begun to alarm Laura, for there were signs that this casual chat down by the herbaceous border was no accident. Since when had Mother trusted her weeding for a start! They both knew she could hardly tell a dahlia from a dandelion. No, this chat was part of a subtle plot to sell the very house they lived in.

'How could you leave your garden?' Laura went on lightly. 'Your hardy annuals would never forgive you, Mother.'

'I think you probably mean hardy perennials. And I can take them with me.'

'You're kidding! You can't sell a house to somebody and leave them an empty garden, can you?'

Victoria Clement waved one of those three-pronged garden fork digger things. Like a little Neptune, thought Laura. 'The man who sold us this house even towed the compost heap away in a trailer! Mind you, we weren't gardeners then so I suppose it hardly mattered. And I don't mean I'd dig up every plant, Laura.'

'What about Daddy's trees? You can't take those with you.'

They both glanced at the pair of young laburnums on either side of the front gate. Visitors often remarked on their graceful weeping form, but in Laura's opinion the trailing branches made the poor things look suicidal.

'And those trees are very important to you, Mummy,' she said slyly. 'They're symbolic.'

Her mother halted a sequence of tidying-up activities to deliver a guarded look. 'Are they indeed? Symbolic of what, exactly?'

'Former times . . . Other days . . . Your previous life when Daddy was alive. We were talking about symbolism in English today – *Macbeth* and all that – and the whole world is absolutely dripping with it from car logos to factory chimneys and it's all unconscious. Or subconscious.'

'I see. You'll be telling me next that Lady Macbeth was a gardener.'

'Don't be ridiculous, she'd have the whole place done in concrete, and quite right, too! And listen to that!' Her mother's kneecaps had cracked in protest as she prised herself off the plastic apron on the grass. 'You're not fit, Mummy, your joints are seizing up and your back's as stiff as a board. If you had to tackle a new garden it would finish you before you finished it.'

This was greeted by a kind of amused snort from her mother, who now appraised the debris in the rickety old wheelbarrow with some satisfaction.

'If I'm such a crock, you can wheel that brute round the back and empty the weeds for me – there's a dear.'

Off she sauntered round the side of the house, twirling Neptune's little trident in a red rubber glove. Her mother had a stately walk, as befits one who has just exercised the power of life and death over the vegetable kingdom, not to mention the occasional fat slug or two. Slugs brought out the Lady Macbeth in her mother's nature. Not only did she tramp on their squelchy bodies without compunction, but she also waged chemical warfare against them. Laura squirmed just thinking about it.

So were they moving house or not? Laura wasn't sure – the entire conversation had been one of ifs and buts and maybes interspersed with the Latin names of plants . . .

'Well, we don't have much room here, do we, Laura? Wouldn't a conservatory be nice, think of early morning tea in the February sun, and do be careful with that ranunculus, it only looks like a buttercup . . .'

Probably it was just a notion she'd got from some glossy mag in the dentist's waiting room, for basically Mother was a settled sort of person, content with her music and her work and her garden. Nothing seemed to annoy her much except for soaps on television (Laura loved them) and she didn't bring home stirring stories of war breaking out in the office.

Or was there more to her mother than met the eye? There surely must be, Laura surmised – there was probably more to every Tom, Dick and Jill than met the eye. Odd, she thought, how I could scribble an essay about that power-crazy psycho Lady Macbeth at the drop of a hat, and yet I could hardly fill a page about my own dear mother.

She grabbed the handles of the wheelbarrow and began to push.

In the kitchen Victoria Clement turned on the cold water tap with the beginnings of a frown upon her face, for she had noticed yet again the fur around the element of the kettle; and once more she found herself lamenting the hardness of the water they were obliged to use in these parts. It never used to be like that, she was sure of it. Heaven alone knew what it was doing to plants and machines and people!

Oh well, she thought, let somebody else write to the papers or complain to the water boards – her days for getting indignant on behalf of worthy causes were over. She plugged in the kettle notwithstanding, and looked out of the window in time to see Laura aiming the wheelbarrow between the upright poles of the rustic arch. One could see, even from the kitchen, that the barrow would ram the arch about one third of the way up on the left-hand side; which it did.

Victoria, identifying with her climbing hydrangea, winced when the blow came, and as the weeds slithered out of the barrow all over Laura's feet, a vulgar word could be heard through the double glazing.

Her daughter would soon be seventeen. Where, right enough, did the years go? In the third drawer down there was an application form, with photo, for her provisional licence. How was that child going to manage a car when she couldn't even steer a wheelbarrow?

The water boiled, the kettle switched itself off. Victoria went to the phone in the hall and put through a call to a Bangor number without consulting her diary. It was one of the few numbers she bothered to retain as a mental fact – had done, from the beginning. Two months ago, was it? Or longer? Thirty years, more like!

'Hello, Jim.'

'Hello, Vicky. Well, how are things?'

'Not so bad. You're back, then.'

'Oh, aye, yesterday. Stayed in a place near Rotterdam. Good food, but windy, mind you. The Dutch know what they're talking about, all right, you have to give credit where it's due.'

How plain his conversation was! You would think to hear him talk that he didn't quite trust the phone, that it existed for the crisp communication of impersonal facts with no words wasted into the bargain.

'Did you miss me, then?' she asked, deliberately crafty.

'Ah, come on! Didn't I twist your arm up your back to come with me?'

The vet, he said, had been out to see one of his sows. The land was too wet, still, to clean out the bottom drain.

'Did you speak to Laura yet?' he asked suddenly.

'Actually . . . No, not yet.'

'Well, you'll have to get round to it sooner or later.'

This had a cantankerous ring to it, but she knew him well enough to make the necessary allowances, had come to feel that he was too used to straight talking and fair dealing to see that there is almost always more than one way of doing things, or that some situations can be complicated in unimagined ways.

'It's not easy for me, Jim, I don't quite know what to say to her.'

'The truth, Vicky.'

'You sound like a Sunday school teacher.'

This slipped out, one of those little jabs one is more entitled to think than to say. All the same, she did not apologise.

'Ah sure, it's easy for me to talk,' he said. 'I'm not the one has to do it.'

'She was helping me just now in the front garden. You should have seen her face when she spiked a worm. It seems I should be more like Lady Macbeth and have the whole place done in concrete.'

It was nice to hear him laugh. They arranged to meet in one of the usual places, and then she put down the phone.

Two

'The circus has arrived in town,' Laura said over her shoulder when she saw the likes of Bucket McKenzie cavorting at the back gate of school. She and Julie had just escaped from a double dose of Physics, only to have their ears assaulted by the mindless hoots and guffaws from the gathering of clowns – their fellow students. The coarser element, as always, was already present in force and tramping over shrubs, jibbering through the railings and generally lacking only lager to turn them into louts.

'What do you think? Somebody's birthday?' Laura asked Julie, who often managed to glean advance notice of such happenings. Not this time, though.

'Dunno. Hey you, Jackson – what's going on here?'

'An auction,' Jackson muttered.

'An auction?' Julie prepared to bully. 'What do you mean an auction – are words being rationed, Jackson, has the

14

government privatised language or do you just need winding up?'

'Bucket's passed his test.'

'Oh my God!' A pair of horror-inflated eyes turned towards Laura. 'Bucket McKenzie's passed his test and that creature shouldn't be allowed to drive a *bike*. I refuse to believe it!'

At that moment, however, willing hands were promoting the horizontal body of Bucket McKenzie to the top of one of the gate pillars, from where he beamed down at his public.

'It was wee buns!' he cried. 'Where's Wilson? Wilson owes me 50p, the skiver.'

As the mob began a maudlin rendering of 'For He's A Jolly Good Fellow' (a lie, of course) Laura heard a sly whisper in her ear.

'Your friend is looking at you romantically across a crowded playground, Miss Clement. Shall you smile back, or shall I?'

Get your radar tuned, Julie, thought Laura. She'd spotted him five moons ago. 'When you smile you scare people, Julie. Anyway, he's only smiling because I smiled first.'

A quick snatch, and Julie had her wrist. 'Huh, no pulse. Laura the parsnip.'

His name was Stephen Kennedy. Their eye contact didn't last long, for a surge of Bucket McKenzie's fans suddenly shunted him backwards into the rhododendrons, out of sight. Julie cried, 'Whoops!' and then giggled.

Nothing had been said between them yet, it was all looks and signals – rather thrilling. And also unexpected. Laura still remembered his maddening goofiness in third form, when Stephen Kennedy had belonged to a manic group of boys whom she and Julie regarded as total idiots and certain to remain so for ever. But then, as Julie was so fond of saying, Biology struck. 'Think what it does for washing powders, Laura! It's all glands and hormones!' Stephen Kennedy had become quite interesting. And interested.

On the other hand there was Bucket McKenzie, whom Biology had turned into an even bigger headache than he'd been back then. His glands and hormones had recently discovered limericks. All you had to do was feed him the first line – 'There

16

was a young lady from Rekjavik . . .' – and pretty soon you had a little poem that would not entice tourists to Iceland. Right now, he was role-playing a Buddha on top of his pillar.

'Roll up, roll up,' he cried, 'one hundred per cent guaranteed unique in the world! Do I hear a bid?'

Julie craned her neck, but failed to see. 'What is he actually selling, that swivel-head?'

'I think he's auctioning his L-plates,' said Laura.

'Used L-plates! He's flogging second-hand L-plates. That is unbelievable.'

The first voice bid 5p.

'Ah, come on, gimme a break, people!'

The second voice bid one hundred thousand pounds.

'Be serious, you lot!' howled Bucket. 'These are lucky plates, you know, these here plates have seen three people through the test – *plus* I will throw in a copy of this book you see in my hand, which is a bestseller, let me tell you.'

'He's flogging his *Highway Code*, Laura,' Julie translated. 'Ask him would he throw in the wheels of his car? Come on, let's get home quick before he starts driving it.'

They crossed the road at the lights and walked side by side down Kingsway Parade until a mini mountain of dog's dirt obliged them to part company.

'So why don't you speak to him?' Julie said. 'Maybe he's shy.'

'Bucket McKenzie?'

'Laura!'

'Patience is a virtue, Julie,' Laura observed lightly.

'Oh well, yes, sure. Patience is fine among *parsnips*.'

'And mind your feet – there's more dog-nitrogen.'

She wanted no fanciful advice from Julie or anyone else on the subject of Stephen Kennedy – she would speak or he would speak in their own sweet time; and anyway, the secret truth of the matter was that she enjoyed their distant understanding, the tingling glances, the resonance that came with the correct timing of a smile. Let Julie go and get swept off her own two feet at one fell swoop if that was how she felt it ought to be.

18

Besides, there weren't too many opportunities to talk naturally because Stephen was an arts student, taking History, French and English, whereas she did English, Physics and Information Technology – an unusual combination, but Mother had insisted on a blend of arts and science subjects. When it looked as though the timetable wouldn't allow such a mixture, Victoria Clement had visited the principal and put him straight about the need for Flexibility in the Modern Curriculum. The very thought of the interview made Laura cringe!

'She's funny this weather,' Laura said. 'I refer to my dear mother, of course.'

'All mothers are funny, Laura, they're allergic to children.'

'Yes, well mine's more allergic than most.'

Only that morning at breakfast her mother had read aloud a poem from the tatty green poetry book she'd had at school – something about the 'still, sad music of humanity' – and she'd been rather shirty when Laura happened to observe that the poem wasn't exactly a bundle of laughs.

'Your mother doesn't read poetry, does she, Julie?'

'She adores the Deaths column in the paper, if that counts.'

'She reads the *Deaths*?'

'Honest. "Wee Timothy's gone, the apple of our eye, but we'll all meet again in the great by and by." And you'd better cut out that laughing because it's sacrilegious and they don't like it up there.'

'You made me laugh, you evil thing!' Laura changed the subject. 'Anyway, the latest is she wants to move house.'

'Where to?'

'Who knows, they seem to be building everywhere you look round here. Why should she suddenly want to live some-where else, that's what I don't understand.'

'Boredom,' stated Julie. 'You wake up some Thursday morning and you're so fed up inside your skull that something's got to change. My dad arrived home one night with a four-metre fish pond for the back garden. Same thing.'

'You haven't got a fish pond,' Laura pointed out.

'Of course we haven't, Mum wouldn't let

him keep it. The thing was one metre deep in the middle, she said somebody's kid would fall in and end up in the Deaths column.' Julie whizzed through her front gate. 'Bye. See you tomorrow, ring if there's News.'

'What news?'

'One never knows,' sang Julie.

Laura took the scenic route home through Barbour Park. The walk gave her time to wonder about Julie's idea of 'boredom'. No doubt it was a terrible force in its own way, but could boredom explain why Mother was still out on the town last night when Laura went to bed at ten to twelve? And the phone calls. Or, rather, the evasiveness after the phone calls – 'Just a friend, Laura, how was school today?' It was all very discreet. Certainly more discreet than a four-metre fish pond.

Or did this behaviour exist in her imagination, really, did you only see what you looked for? Could anybody seem routine when they made you study out-and-out loopers like Lady Macbeth, for heaven's sake! She began to think of Stephen Kennedy. Remembering how he looked at her sometimes, she found herself smiling at strangers and their dogs.

Three

It was well after four when Laura got home and began to tidy up the kitchen in the manner approved by Mother: cups placed high, saucers low, pans under the sink – for all the world like the precise notes in that dreary music her mother sang. If the score said F sharp you sang F sharp or you gummed up the works. Same with cups and saucers, they had their particular place to be like all the little crotchets and quavers. Same with washing on the line – hang this one by the waistband, that one by the armpits and the others upside down. Laura emptied the dishwasher.

This was the art of being 'organised'. People often said, 'How wonderfully organised you always are, Victoria,' and Laura, who could hardly read a note of music any more and whose bedroom was a shambles, reflected wryly about the problem with people who are 'organised': they forced other people to be organised, too.

The last item she came to on the almost-cleared surfaces was the green book with his lordship Wordsworth in it. Now here was a puzzle. Where in the tidy scheme of things did one place a relic that was pushing thirty years of age? Flicking open the cover, she saw the name VICTORIA STIRLING written there above a quotation in her mother's teenage cursive:

> 'Know Thyself, for there is no land
> so far removed from you, nor one
> about which you will so easily
> believe falsehoods.'

Mag rack, Laura decided.

She had stuck the book between the *Radio Times* and a brochure about Victorian conservatories when the key turned in the lock.

'Hi, Mum. Buy anything exciting on the way home?'

'I don't buy clothes on the way home, Laura, I buy things like bread and butter and frozen vegetables. What are you grinning at?'

'The bare necessities. Get it?'

'Get what?'

24

'It's a song, Mummy – "The Bare Necessities."'

Her mother whipped out a large, frozen gateau. 'Well, there's another one. You haven't forgotten Peggy's coming tomorrow evening?' An eyebrow rose as she pirouetted. 'Nice tidy kitchen. Home long?'

'A while. I was talking to Julie about moving house today. I think she reckons it would be fun.'

'Julie would. Julie thinks life ought to be one long afternoon in the amusement arcade. Set out a knife and fork each while I nip out to the freezer, there's a dear.'

Laura obliged, and met her mother with a question as she came through the back door. 'If we did move, say to one of those new houses on Moat Road, would I be able to have my room the way I want it?'

'Haven't you always?'

'No, Mother, I haven't always. I want a phone in my room and you won't let me have it.'

'Oh, là là,' said her mother, *comme les Français,* 'when I was your age we didn't have a phone at all – however did we manage!'

'You had carrier pigeons.'

'Exactly. We wrote letters, which is a very elegant method of communication.'

'Elegant but outmoded, Mother,' Laura said, cunningly distributing cork mats higgledy-piggledy on the table-top (Mother liked parallel lines and right angles). 'When you think about it, modern information technology and all that, the phone is a bit of a dinosaur already. It belongs to the electronic stone age. Ask anybody, they'll tell you.'

'Well, I have to pay the phone bill with a good old-fashioned thing called money, so one phone will do us for the time being.'

When the doorbell rang Laura darted into the hall to answer it, leaving her mother to straighten the table mats. On the step stood a young fellow hardly older than herself. Not that she took time to notice him, for he was bearing flowers.

What a splash! He spoke from behind a dozen carnations, pink and white with fiddly ferny bits to make it all fuzzily romantic.

'Delivery to 18 Ashfield Manor Mews. Are you Clement?'

'Yes! Gimme them,' said Laura.

'Mrs Victoria Clement?'

'Look, she's my mother, OK?'

'Bet you thought they were for you.' And away he went, the cheeky thing, after having the nerve to wink at her.

Laura returned to the kitchen, crowing. 'Look what came, out of nowhere, aren't they beauties!'

Her mother gaped like a goldfish. 'Good glory! How spectacular. You must have an admirer.'

'Don't be ridiculous, Mummy, the people I know wouldn't buy me flowers for my funeral. These gorgeous things are all for you. And there's a card.'

It was strange how her mother failed to take up the excitement of the moment. After half a step forward she stopped, and simply stared.

'Well . . . Are you sure?'

'It says, "From Jim" and I only know one Jim. Believe me, he's not the type, I've seen his tattoos.'

'Heavens above!'

Her mother, who never fiddled, fiddled now with her string of Majorcan pearls.

'You've lost your cool, Mum, which is understandable, of course – you wouldn't be the first person to be momentarily unnerved by an unexpected bolt from the blue.'

Now she took the flowers. 'Oh, stop your twittering on, Laura, and reach me down that vase.'

'One vase. I reckon they cost a fortune, but somebody obviously thinks you're worth it. Who is this Jim person, then?'

'Have you ever heard of a thing called minding your own business, Laura?'

'I believe in the frank and open exchange of views, Mother.'

'You do when it suits you.' There was a pause while the vase filled with water. 'Anyway, you've met him once or twice. Jim Mulholland.'

Laura tried to search and recall, but the effort simply turned her mind into a blank.

'He let us sit in his Range Rover,' Mother prompted, 'at a show some time back. It was raining.'

'Was Granny Stirling with us?'

'Yes.'

A lumbering shape came into her mind,

28

dressed in a green waxed coat, wellies, tweed cap . . . Memory rushed in to colour the outline, but could not supply a face. There had been mud . . .

'That farmer? Mother, you cannot be serious. That farmer sent you roses?'

'Carnations, Laura. And I appreciate them, let me assure you.'

'He was at one of your concerts, then? Is this a floral tribute, did he hear you sing?'

'It's a bunch of flowers, that's what it is.'

Some bunch! she thought. 'Well, does this mean that there is a romantic attachment going on behind my back?'

Her mother smiled a maddening smile at the head of parsley she happened to be shredding into minuscule bits for a fish sauce. 'That imagination will run away with you one day. Do something useful, please – like start those two fish for the tea.'

The tea was a nonchalant affair. Mother sat there looking as cool and fresh as parsley, and described the potential of the latest computer she was working with before rising to turn on the local radio news. This was part of her routine, and she did it in case someone she knew had been killed. It was so like Julie's mother's fixation with the Deaths column that Laura wondered if you got hooked on that sort of thing when you saw the number 40 looming on the horizon. The still sad music of humanity. Not a word was said about flowers or farmers.

Not that she, Laura, had anything against farmers, but nobody in her right mind could argue that they had the most dynamic image in the world – Hollywood didn't make movies about farmers, they were a totally anonymous class of people who went about driving tractors and Range Rovers and making money. What a turn-up! None of this fitted in with the crotchets and the quavers.

Then she remembered something. The Mulhollands were big farming people around Bangor, near where Granny Stirling still lived, he must be the same connection. Probably her mother had known him for donkeys, maybe they'd grown up together, climbed the same country trees, played chasing in the school playground . . .

She didn't dare ask. There had been an excuse for the third degree in the heat of the moment, but Laura could see that *she* wouldn't want Mother bombarding her with a lot of fool questions about Stephen Kennedy; and what was sauce for the goose was sauce for the gosling, so to speak.

Julie was a different matter, though. She would have to be phoned.

Shortly after tea the piano began to sound out in the small room – a sure sign that Mother would be launching her voice into something by one of those Italian names ending with an 'i'. Millions of them, all scribbling operas, and now the Italians were more crazy about football. Giggling over the idea of opera-hooligans and picking up the phone, Laura launched into an unexpurgated account of the whole incident.

Julie's first words were, 'I bet you thought they were for you.'

'I've been through that, Julie, with the goon who brought them, right? And don't tell me it's not peculiar. How many farmers send people carnations?'

'Well, it's food for thought all right, but maybe he grows carnations, maybe they're seconds out of his greenhouse.'

'He's a pig farmer, Julie.'

'There you are, then. He couldn't very well send her a side of bacon, could he?'

'Julie!'

'What's he like?'

'Oh, Lord, what's he like!'

There he was in her mind's eye waddling through the muck like a duck in wellies, following a big fat pig called Luigi. Luigi wore a green rosette near his floppy ear – some other pig had beaten him to first place in the beauty competition or whatever.

'He's got this shock of red hair, it's like something you'd glue on a rag doll. And their house is huge.'

'Sounds like money, Laura. Is there any . . .'

'Hanky-panky, do you mean?'

'No, that's what I didn't mean. But is there?'

'Well, I don't know. I've never seen him in this house but that proves . . . Hang on!' The music had stopped next door, but only for a change of key or tune or whatever. '. . . That doesn't prove anything. I've never seen him in this house but there's always his place in the back of beyond.'

'Calm down, Laura, your mother's forty.'

'Thirty-nine. And it was you who mentioned hanky-panky.'

A lusty laugh travelled down the phone. 'I have never called it hanky-panky in my whole life, Laura dear, and if I was you I'd update my vocab. What about the card – did it say from Jim with love or anything like that?'

'No, just his name.'

'There you are then. Roses are different, they stand for passion. If a fellow sends you a single red rose it means he can't eat and can't sleep and all that's keeping him alive is sweet memories of you. It's his actual heart he's giving you, you know.'

Laura felt like asking Julie where she gathered up all her rubbish from, but didn't have time.

'And quit worrying. You told me yourself that your mum's always bringing home little gifts, she's Victoria Clement, the opera singer. Look at the skaters on TV, flowers all over the ice at the drop of a hat and all it means is well done, chaps, you put on a jolly good show.'

'But she blushed, Julie!'

'Good sign! Only the innocent blush, I read that some place. Think about it. I bet old "Is this a dagger I see before me" never blushed in her life. Right?'

Laura appeared to be croaking her last at the foot of the stairs when her mother emerged from the small room and levelled an inquisitive glance at her.

'You seem to be having fun.'

'It's Julie, Mum. She'd keep you in stitches, you know what she's like. She said something interesting. "Only the innocent blush." '

Her mother's head tilted – not without a touch of appreciation, Laura thought. But her mother said, 'Whether one is innocent or guilty hasn't got much to do with it. It depends primarily on how close the blood vessels are to the skin.'

'Oh. I see.' Laura nodded wisely.

Four

From some way off Laura saw Julie and Stephen Kennedy sitting together on the low stone wall at the front of the school. Julie had perhaps treated him to one of her amusing little anecdotes, for Stephen appeared to be laughing, and one of his arms was clamped curiously across his chest, as if to protect his wallet from a pickpocket. Or give himself a one-armed hug. Or maybe Julie was trying to tickle him. At one point their bodies swayed so close that only a glimmer of daylight separated them – and this had better *not* be hanky-panky, thought Laura.

They didn't see her approaching. Laura found herself wondering about that jaunty glitter of Julie's infectious conversation – how could she ever match that talent for talking, and where did it come from? How did you get it? Big families? Julie was the third of five children and her stories of home life were full of blood, guts, love, intestines and happiness.

'Laura! Oh wait until you hear this, but you'll never believe it. Show her what you've gone and done, Stevie Kennedy.'

'No! And give me back my *Highway Code*.'

Julie made a dive for the inside pocket of his jacket, but he fought her off with a look of happy determination on his face. This interlude of horseplay, during which they bounced off one another shamelessly, ended when Julie sat back, defeated, and adjusted her dress demurely.

'Keep them, then. The screwball paid Bucket McKenzie for his tatty old L-plates and he already has L-plates of his own. But of course he's probably a secret multi-billionaire.'

'They're lucky L-plates,' Stephen said. 'Those plates have seen five people through the test.' And he glanced at Laura, who smiled, but not generously.

'Oh, *five* now, is it,' declared Julie. 'The last I heard it was only three. Why don't you try offering up a prayer to somebody up there?'

'I might do that too. I need all the help I

can get.'

'When is the big day, Stephen?' Laura asked quietly.

She said his name in full, and she said it warmly. It was a serious question, and she waited for an answer. She was conscious of creating a new emphasis in the conversation: a patch of common ground among the zany quicksands where good sense could prevail. She did it deliberately. Julie was thrust aside as a mere entertainer.

'Pretty soon, actually.'

'And he's not telling us when in case he fails and we slag him for being a dodo! That's not very positive thinking, Stevie, you mustn't be afraid of failure.'

'Julie believes that you should meet failure halfway,' Laura said sweetly, smiling just enough to conceal the barb.

Not from him, though. He threw a glance at her then, condoning her crafty remark with a knowing grin. A glance, a look, a stare . . . she saw the smile simply wither on his face, a victim of Biology. This is the public street! Laura reminded herself.

'OK!' said Julie, flicking through the *Highway Code*. 'Let's see who knows his onions. When are you allowed to doot your horn? Stevie?'

'What?'

'Horns! When can you use them?'

'To let people know you're there.'

'I'll accept that. You're lucky I'm feeling lenient. What should you do when you see a chicken crossing the road? Well?'

'It doesn't say that.'

'Page thirty, in black and white, and this just isn't good enough. Here comes your last chance or you fail, so concentrate. What speed was Banquo doing in his Ferrari when he appeared to Macbeth as a ghost?'

As Stephen Kennedy, stern as a bailiff, repossessed his *Highway Code*, and while Julie snorted, squealed and wriggled in his grasp, Laura allowed the giddy lightness of the previous moment to bubble out of her mouth – for all the world as though the idea of Banquo's ghost driving a Ferrari had left her helpless.

Someone called her name above the thunder of a passing lorry; and, turning, she caught a glimpse of her mother on the other side of the road.

'Oh, no, I forgot she was meeting me! I'd

better run or I'm dead, you two.' She tried to think of something snappy and meaningful to say to him, but couldn't.

'Goodbye, Stephen.'

'My God,' cried Julie, ' "goodbye" she says. Are you emigrating?'

'Only shopping,' called Laura, dancing down the pavement. 'We're entertaining tonight and I'm doing the cooking.'

'Irish stew?'

'Lasagne – peasant!'

From their side of the road Julie and Stephen Kennedy observed Laura ford the gush of traffic and meet up with her mother on the far side. When Mrs Clement waved a hand on that distant shore, Julie returned it with good measure. Stephen's hand flickered self-consciously, as if he wasn't quite sure that he had been included in the wave and was therefore entitled to reply.

'That's Laura's mother?' he said.

'Yes, why?'

'Well . . . I just thought she'd look older, that's all. You know what I mean. She's quite good-looking, isn't she?'

'Listen to me, Stevie Kennedy,' said Julie, assuming the manner of a consultant in matters of delicacy, 'that is Victoria Clement, she *sings*, and believe me we are talking high notes here, not your hard rock or soul – she's much too sophisticated for working-class yobbos like some I could mention without pointing any elbows. Mind you,' came an afterthought, 'you've got to admire her, it can't have been easy when you think about it.'

'What are you talking about?'

'Her husband. He was killed in a booby-trap explosion.'

'Laura's dad? They blew him up?'

'Mistaken identity. They apologised, of course. Nice of them.'

'When?'

'She was about four or five, I think.' Julie emphasised her vagueness with a shrug. 'A long time.'

'Jeez, I never knew.'

'It's not exactly light conversation, is it? She never talks about it, so watch what you say and don't put your big banana foot in it, Stevie Kennedy. OK?'

Five

The flowers had been a goad, of course, in the literal sense of that rather quaint word: a tool to get something moving. Victoria Clement had realised this fact as soon as the bouquet arrived – had experienced, indeed, a metaphorical kick on the rump as soon as she'd set eyes on them. 'Get cracking, Vicky,' those flowers had chirped, 'the time has come to speak of many things. Tell her.'

And exactly why she wouldn't tell Laura, or couldn't bring herself to tell her, Victoria had no idea. It wasn't as if she had difficulty in being direct with people, for being direct with people was part and parcel of her work in financial services. Sometimes she opened a client's ledgers and read between the lines – or, at least, between the figures – that here was a business in a state of terminal decline: a haemorrhage of lost money, lost time, lost prestige, lost hope. Oh yes, sometimes she could be direct to the point of causing misery.

With the flowers had arrived the perfect opportunity, so why hadn't she taken it? It must mean that she was not completely sure even yet. This was not like her.

'Mummy! Why are you holding that vase, you look like a statue.'

The question came from the direction of the cooker, where Laura stood wearing an oven glove.

'I'm wondering where to put it.'

'Well, are we sure that Peggy likes cheese?'

'Yes. At least . . . In any case it's too late, we're not having lasagne without cheese, especially not for Peggy Osborne.'

'She eats in the best hotels, doesn't she, Mum?'

'Yes, dear, Peggy often says that she eats in the best hotels.'

Victoria smiled to think how Peggy would be awarding marks out of ten tonight from the moment when she picked up her serviette. But then, why else were they having her? They hadn't invited her along to plonk a plate in her lap – everyone needed at least one friend who expected you to live up to their standards, and there was no point in resenting Peggy for being herself. A lot of people did, of course.

As a simple precaution, though, Victoria moved the vase of flowers into a bedroom. They would only titillate Peggy's curiosity beyond endurance.

She needn't have bothered. The evening was to be a disaster.

Peggy leaned back in her seat, smiled with her rather wide, loose lips, and declared that she was not one to mince her words about food – that lasagne had been absolutely delicious. And she'd no idea that Victoria had gone all Italian all of a sudden, and with such panache, and to produce that Tuscan wine, well it was too exquisite, too cruel – too devilishly insightful, for it made her want to cry for all the summers that would never come again.

You have no notion of crying, thought Victoria. 'Why thank you, Peggy,' she said, 'but I didn't make it. Laura did it all.'

'Did you, Laura? Glory be to heaven, child, you're only a treasure!'

The humble Laura muttered something about not choosing the music or the wine.

But Peggy was in the mood to praise. 'Nonsense! And you didn't learn to cook like that out of a book, of that I'm certain. And I know, because I've tried and I remain very average, as they say. What are you laughing at, Victoria?'

'At you, Peggy. Modesty doesn't suit you.'

'Oh, I've never minded being modest among friends. You must have a flair for it, Laura. Of course it's only right that girls can do science and all that sort of thing nowadays, but really, there's something to be said for good, old-fashioned cookery classes.'

'She doesn't do cookery, Peggy, she does English, Physics and Information Technology.'

'Information Technology? What *is* that? No, don't tell me, I don't want to know. It's computers, isn't it? I never talk about machines!'

With care, Victoria filled Peggy's glass to the point where it could be lifted and laid without accident, and they smiled at one another with wine-dark teeth. Another success. If the wine didn't darken your teeth

Peggy assumed that it came from the Balkans.

'One must move with the times, Peggy.'

'One musn't do any such thing. And it's making the generation gap a hundred times worse than ever it was. We soon won't know what young people are talking about if nobody puts a stop to all this. Isn't there something in what I'm saying, Laura?'

'The same applies to me and music, Mrs Osborne. I don't understand what you and Mum see in your opera, it's all gloom and doom.'

'Dear me.' Peggy sighed. 'Is there no hope for her, Victoria?'

None. She was suddenly reminded of the brief battle she'd had with her daughter some years ago over piano lessons: Laura, pleading boredom with the whole process, had won in the end. The child had been a passable player in a wooden sort of way, but there was no spark there, no feeling. It would have been worse had she been passionately keen on the piano, for the talent just wasn't there.

'I did my best,' Victoria said. 'How are rehearsals going, Peggy? Everyone in good voice? No fits of pique?'

'Not yet, but then we haven't started casting. When that happens pique will be rampant, I assure you. George Adams is producing us this year. Good musically, of course, but . . . well, let's just say he has his weaknesses. I heard him say he wants you for *The Gondoliers*, Victoria.'

'I don't think so, Peggy. Not this year.'

'Why not, Mum?' Laura asked, curious.

'Why not, indeed?' cried Peggy. 'We're a small company, Victoria, talent is thin on the ground. And to hear George Adams talk anyone would think we were bound for the Albert Hall, no less. We need all the experience we can get to keep that man's head out of the clouds.'

'You know how things are,' said Victoria. 'Actually I talked to George on the phone and told him I had . . . other commitments.'

'Other commitments. Oh, I see, that's still going on, is it? I'm warning you, Victoria Clement, we won't be pleased if and when you run off to live in Bangor at the drop of a hat. You might as well take yourself off to Tasmania or the dark side of the moon for all we'll see of you *then*.'

Victoria said, 'Who would like coffee?' but the damage had been done. There was scarcely a pause before Laura pounced.

'What do you mean "run off to Bangor", what are you talking about?'

'Peggy isn't talking about anything, Laura, she's just talking.'

'She said you were moving to Bangor. That's nearly fifty miles away.'

The blunt fact produced an odd silence, which in turn was pointed up by the music in the background. An aria from *Maria Stuarda*. They might almost have been listening to it, all three.

'No I didn't say that, I said . . .'

'Be quiet, Peggy. This isn't the time, Laura.'

'This isn't the time for what? You're trying to keep something from me, Mother. What did she mean about moving to Bangor?'

Peggy said, 'I was just making ordinary conversation. Ordinary conversation. I don't know anything about anything . . .' but her blustering effort petered out as she sat back to stare somewhat wide-eyed at

Laura, who had risen from the table.

'You want to sell everything we've got and move to Bangor!'

'We can talk about this later,' Victoria said, calmly, although she was also surprised by the child's uninhibited intensity. Unusual.

'You obviously have, you've talked about it already! You can talk about it to other people, they know everything and I know nothing, but then I'm just the one who lives here. Well, you can talk about it from now to Christmas for all I care because I can tell you now what I have to say, Mother. I am not going.'

These last four words were delivered from the door with ominous calm; then she was gone. Exit stage left, Victoria thought absurdly, pursued by a bear.

'End of pleasant evening, I suggest,' she said to her guest.

'Victoria, I feel so stupid.'

'These things happen, Peggy.'

'I'm shattered. I thought she must surely know by now.'

'I'm afraid you didn't think at all, Peggy, but like I say, we'll all get over it. How about coffee and a biscuit?'

'I couldn't help it, you know me. And two glasses of wine . . . I thought she must know.'

'Why?'

'Why? Well . . . She's your daughter, Victoria.'

Poor Peggy! The burden of trying to understand was so plain on her face that Victoria reached out and lightly touched the back of her hand. 'It's my fault, too. I should have been more free and easy about all this, of course I should, but I'm not. The natural diffidence is there – I can't deny it and I don't know why. You see, Peggy, I won't ever ask Laura if she's sleeping with her boyfriend and *my* relationship with Jim Mulholland is private, too. She has no divine right to know about it until I choose to tell her.'

Peggy said, somewhat timidly, 'But she does live here, Laura. You'll have to take her with you.'

'Yes, I know. And it'll be a shock to her system, I see that now. I know, I know. All the same, she's sixteen and God knows, Peggy, she's no hot-house plant that's

49

going to droop when the first cold wind blows! And if there's one thing I cannot stand it's a fit of adolescent pique.' Conscious that her voice had risen, Victoria made an effort to smile. '*Would* you like some coffee?'

'I think I'd better go, don't you? Tell Laura the meal was just delightful, will you, and I'm sorry for being such a fool.'

'It's all right, Peggy. And don't annoy yourself. I was going to tell her, really, but somehow . . . it's not easy. We haven't got that kind of closeness, we don't cuddle up and tell all. I'll get your coat.'

'Huh! The thing's done, it's only fit for Oxfam. One is so wary of all the fuss about wearing fur these days.'

Peggy was returning to normal. At the door Victoria said, 'Give my love to George Adams.'

'Oh, don't talk. You know what he told me the other day? He says he's a member of the Slim Whitman Appreciation Society, and I wouldn't put it past him!'

Victoria Clement laughed. 'He's pulling your leg, Peggy. Goodnight.'

Six

The dinner debris having spread over two rooms, Victoria adhered to her general principles of chaos management by clearing the dining room first and then setting about the kitchen. She wondered from time to time whether the sound of activity might shame Laura out of her room, but thought it unlikely. There had been too much drama in the scene for that to happen, and she would have to go down there and break the ice. Break it, and avoid falling into the hole.

How ironic it was that after Bob died she had been more determined than ever to make her daughter into an independent person; an individual. With the strength not to cling to her! On tonight's evidence, Laura had no intention of clinging. 'I can tell you now, Mother – I am not going.' What on earth was she going to say, how would she begin? Victoria hated this business in her heart.

With tragedy she could cope – had been

obliged – but she had no time for those petty, self-indulgent squabbles of the domestic kind that were reported to her, verbatim, during coffee breaks at work. 'So I said to her and she said to me and I wasn't letting him get away with *that*, I can tell you . . .' There came to mind, as she put away a dish, a colleague who claimed that she could reduce her husband to tears in ten minutes. And if you lift the phone tomorrow, Victoria had almost said, and they tell you his car's shapeless, and he's inside it just as shapeless, unrecognisable – which one of you will have the last laugh in the little games you play? Frankly, such brawling was beneath her dignity; there would be no quarrelling with Laura.

But what should she do, then? Ignoring the situation was no longer an option. It would be nice, she thought, to have someone there to talk it all over with, but that was an old and treacherous feeling that she understood too well. You knew where the buck stopped in a one-parent family.

She stacked the pots on the draining board, preferring to leave them until tomorrow. Then she switched on the machine and went down the hall to Laura's room.

The important thing was to be consistent. She would be firm, relaxed and direct. More than direct – she would be truthful. Twice she knocked, and went in.

'Peggy has gone home. She asked me to tell you that the meal was wonderful. Which it was.'

'You've told me, OK.'

Flick. A page turned in the pool of light from the bedside lamp. The ends of her dangling hair, too, glowed in the light, and the whole pose of her lying on the bed suggested a monumental indifference to anything she might have to listen to.

'This is not a good idea, Laura. Running away to sulk in your room doesn't suit you at all. I'm putting on the kettle, do you want a cup?'

'No thanks.'

'Perhaps you'd like something brought to you here?'

'Look, you needn't try to smooth-talk over things, Mummy, I'm not interested and I understand everything, so let me sulk in peace if that's what you think I'm doing.'

'It's much more likely,' Victoria said in a

measured way, 'that at your age you understand a lot less than you think.'

The book slammed shut. 'At least I understand why Victoria Clement won't be singing Gilbert and Sullivan this year, she's much too busy reading brochures about Victorian conservatories and towing away compost heaps. And those flowers!'

Victoria sat down cautiously, as if the bed were suspect. 'Jim Mulholland sent me those flowers because he has strong feelings for me and has had for many years.'

'Well, what do you expect me to say about that?'

'I don't know. I've never known what I expect you to say about that.' Hide nothing, a still voice said, not even the awkwardness of talking about it. 'I knew from the beginning that this would be a difficult subject for us.'

'Are you telling me that he fancied you when Daddy was alive?'

She shook her head. Actually the answer was yes, but irrelevant. 'You don't remember your father, do you?'

'Yes I do. What's that got to do with it?'

'I just want you to understand that I

remember everything about him, and I always will. I hadn't fully realised, you see, that when a person dies he doesn't necessarily go away all at once, not entirely. You don't want him to, either. It sounds macabre, but it isn't.'

'If you say so.'

'I used to ask his advice sometimes, even though he . . . wasn't there, of course. Should I go away on holiday, take out insurance, send you to the prep. school, paper the lounge? Curious, really. We even talked out loud.'

'You sound as if you're round the bend, Mother.'

'Very likely. But all that passed. I didn't feel very much about anyone for a long time. And now there's Jim Mulholland.'

The mention of his name brought her to a kind of unnatural pause between what had been said, and what was yet to come. And all this talk, this knowledge, she thought, this ancient history, this unveiling of her mental constructs that she so much hated to unveil – what was it for? But hide nothing. Her voice quickened. 'It isn't very easy for me to speak of personal matters, Laura, but

55

your father knew Jim, and I know he would rather I got together with that good, quiet man than spend the rest of my life cluttering up yours – and ultimately coming to depend on you absolutely, of course.'

'So we're moving to Bangor for my benefit, are we?'

She rose from the bed, allowing a measure of anger to flare in her voice. 'Dammit, Laura, I won't let you deliberately mis-understand me. I'll be like your Granny Stirling some day, that's what I'm saying. And in six or five years' time or less, you will come along and tell me whom you are marrying, and when. You won't ask me – you'll *tell* me. And if I don't like it, you'll say – tough. And I'm not asking you now, I am telling you how my life is going to be. Goodnight.'

She made a point of waiting at the bedroom door, forcing her daughter to make a civil reply. Which duly came. 'Goodnight.'

Seven

'It's almost official, by the way. We're moving house.'

'To Moat Road or Dunwoody Court?'

'Try Bangor.'

'Sugar, Laura, you are kidding me!'

'The flowers, the flowers, I told you they meant business. So much for single red roses and beating hearts.'

'I was having a good day until now,' wailed Julie. 'Somebody always, always, always drops a load of nitrogen on my *Thursdays.*'

They were standing under the dome of 'Piccadilly Circus', that point in the new school buildings where five corridors merged and brought together students from the arts and sciences and the social sciences in order to promote, presumably, a mighty concourse of ideas. What you actually got during the afternoon break was a vast acoustic gossip shop. Laura found herself shouting out highly confidential information at the top of her voice.

'I honestly think she must be cracking up, Julie. I've never seen my mother like this before. Never.'

'She doesn't look any different, well, Stevie thought she was your sister yesterday, which doesn't prove a thing of course because if you ask me men spend half their lives looking at women and never notice details, right? But she *was* looking well. Must be all that singing high notes.' Julie attempted high doh. Nobody turned a hair, such was the volume of noise from the trivia traffic.

'You should have seen her last night, standing cool as ice in my doorway. "I'm not asking you, Laura, I am telling you how my life is going to be." I felt like the family poodle. She still talks to my dad as if he's a ghost, you know. And the thing is he answers back.'

'Pure Shakespeare,' Julie observed professorially. 'People were always seeing ghosts, it was the done thing. Only candles, you see. What are we going to do, Laura? You just can't go to Bangor, you'll end up talking to trees! Oh, get lost!'

This was addressed to the school bell,

which grated on regardless from on high, higher than a person could reach – higher than a person could reach standing on another person's shoulders with chewing gum in one's hand. It had been tried.

Thursday was Julie's badminton day. Laura walked home alone that afternoon: up Kingsway, a right at Moat Road, left fork at the Esso garage or the right fork, either route took her into Ashfield Avenue, then across the road into the Mews. The entire walk home had such a shape to it that she didn't even have to think about it.

But when she did, then, think about it, the sudden familiarity of the place was startling. She had knowledge of quirky house names, of fancy chimneys, a conifer shaped like a duck, new aerials and squarials and gutted front gardens where cars now stood on three-by-two pavers. Blindfolded, without seeing, she would know the house with the two stone griffins from the one with the lion's head in the wrought-iron gate, she could pluck a crisp bag or a can from the depths of Stephensons' privet hedge. The special knowledge she had of this place made it hers, part of her mental landscape, her patch, home. She had never been struck before by the significance of place.

And people? How many friends did a person have? Laura saw that she dare not allow herself to think of the significance of people. It wouldn't do to arrive home pinky-eyed and blotchy, for Mother had always been unimpressed by tears. 'I know it's not fair, Laura, but the world's not fair, so there, there, blow your nose and soldier on . . .' Somewhat viciously Laura twisted the key in the lock and went in. Thank God the place was empty. She wandered about enjoying the heavenly respite of absolute privacy and ignored the leaning tower of Pisa on the draining board.

She'd hardly been in the house five minutes before the doorbell sounded and she discovered Stephen Kennedy standing on her doorstep. In a blue sweater, open-necked shirt, jeans and soft shoes, clutching a paper bag. Bright-eyed and jumpy-looking. All this she saw in the first flush of astonishment.

'Hello,' he said.

'Hello yourself. Come in.'

'No, I was just passing and I thought I'd drop these in for you.'

The slim paper bag in his hand gave a little flutter.

'Stephen, will you come in a minute, there's nobody here to eat you.'

He's been home and changed already, she thought. His hair was slightly damp after washing and swept back so that he looked . . . what was that word? . . . aero-dynamic. And fresh and nice and lovely. His darting blue eyes met hers, but not like yesterday, because you could tell that he still felt there might be cannibals behind the curtains. Once through the door she steered him towards the kitchen, stooping to pick up a letter which had been caught behind the doormat. It had a Bangor postmark. How elegant, she thought, sticking it between the pages of his lordship Wordsworth.

'You don't mind me calling, then?'

'I don't mind. You know I don't mind.'

'I didn't see you in school today,' Stephen said, as if she suffered from bouts of invisibility.

'Well, I didn't see you either. Tea or coffee?'

'Have you any strawberry cordial?'

'What?'

'It's red stuff,' he explained seriously, 'you put it in milk and . . . It doesn't matter, Laura. I'm pushed for time, actually. Driving lesson.'

'Isn't it a bit close to teatime?'

'It's the last one before the test and he wants to take me through heavy traffic.'

'When is it?'

'Tomorrow. I brought you these.'

She drew out of the paper bag a pair of shining new plastic L-plates. Strawberry cordial, she realised, had just been promoted to the top of the shopping list.

'Maybe you've got them already?' he said.

'I haven't,' she lied. 'They're wonderful. I wouldn't swop these L-plates for Bucket McKenzie's, honest!'

And when you get your test, Laura wanted to add, I'd better be the first girl you take out in the car. She thought: I certainly won't be the last after we move to Bangor.

He came closer, close enough to dance. 'I just wanted to say something.'

'Oh?' Laura swallowed. He looked

deadly serious. Could she handle this?

'About Bucket's lucky plates. I didn't really buy them, you know, I was only joking with Julie that time. I wouldn't want you to think I was superstitious. Why are you smiling?'

'Nothing,' she said. 'Will you call me and tell me if you pass? I'll give you my number.'

'Well, I know it, actually.' And he blushed. 'You don't mind? I'd like to know about you, Laura.'

She was his third A level! English, History and Laura Clement! '*Will* you call me?'

He nodded. Perhaps he took her hands or she took his – either way they touched at last, and right on cue her mother came through the door. Her glance seemed to ping off Stephen to the column of last night's dishes and back again, but there was only surprise on her face, nothing more.

'Stephen Kennedy, Mum. Stephen, this is my mother.'

They shook hands. Mother was flowing, radiant and correct; Stephen appeared to have joints like Pinocchio.

'Hello, Stephen, you're very welcome. I assume you're one of Laura's friends from school.'

During the wash of words about school and career choices that followed, Laura slid the L-plates into a drawer in case her mother let slip that she already had a pair. They were talking about journalism when Laura interrupted.

'Stephen has to go, Mummy, he's got a driving lesson in the rush-hour traffic.'

'Oh, dear!' Mother said grandly. 'In at the deep end!'

Laura took his hand and led him out of the room, just to show that he was something she had shares in, so to speak. Mother would take note.

'Good luck, then,' she said at the door.

'Thanks. I hope I don't get the examiner with a moustache, he's supposed to be a brute.'

'I'm glad you called.'

He smiled at her and then didn't smile, his face close to hers, the refracted image of the angled door shining for a moment in the liquid lights of his eyes before he moved away.

'I'll expect a lift home tomorrow, then?'

'*If*!' he shouted back, giving the thumbs-down sign.

Laura suddenly decided that she would not return to the kitchen and help with whatever remained to be done. Instead she went into the lounge and turned on the TV – a sort of unstructured deviation from their normal way of going, but one that was consistent with the atmosphere created by the events of last evening. There had been a coolness at breakfast that morning, a coolness that she wanted to preserve until she had had her say.

She had things to say to her mother.

Bugs Bunny was on. Before long her mother appeared at the door of the lounge.

'Well, Laura, you look comfortable. How were things today? Did you get your essay back?'

'No, she hasn't marked it yet. Mr King had odd socks on again and Margaret Lapsley got through to a spirit on the ouija board last night. It was French. Said it knew Napoleon.'

'It all sounds very intellectually stimulating. Like Bugs Bunny.'

'I like Bugs Bunny. So does Julie. Everybody likes Bugs Bunny.'

'He's a rabbit,' said Mother.

'There's a letter for you in Wordsworth.'

'It can wait until after we've tidied up.'

'Until you can read it in private, you mean. I've been thinking about what you said last night, Mother, about life. I think you left somebody out of all the plans you seem to be making. Me.'

Her mother perched on the edge of a lounge chair – the sit of someone who does not expect to be detained for long. And yet she seemed to welcome the opportunity to speak.

'Yes . . . I've been thinking, too, and I'm not sure that I was entirely fair to either of us in the way I expressed myself. I was annoyed at Peggy for her . . . premature disclosure, shall we say. I wanted to tell you myself, and would have soon. And I was annoyed at you for leaving the table the way you did. I ended up being annoyed at myself, if it helps.'

It didn't help. Laura pulled her legs under her, making a tight knot of herself in the chair.

'I'm still saying that you left me out. What about me, don't I have a say?'

'I didn't leave you out, Laura. I'm aware that this is going to cause some short-term problems for you, but . . .'

'But your problems are more important than mine?' Laura zapped the rabbit with the remote control. 'Don't you understand that there are people in my life too that I can't bear to be without?'

'But I'm thinking several years ahead . . .'

'I'm not!' Her body unwound itself in the creaking leather chair. 'When will I see my friends, how will I get to youth council meetings? I'm facing total, absolute upheaval and annihilation here, new school, new uniform, I'll be one of the kids who gets out early for the country bus, new teachers, new *daddy*!'

'Laura . . .'

'You're rubbing out every single thing I've grown up with but I'm not going.'

That, more or less, was the case she had intended to put, though she had not anticipated putting it with quite so much passion, or leaving herself quite so breathless – like one of those tennis players who need to curse umpires and break racquets before they start hitting aces. Her mother, too, was flushed.

'Don't be so foolish and dramatic. Believe me, you'll fit into a new way of going more easily than you ever imagine. You're not afraid of people – you've never been afraid of meeting new people!'

'How do you know what I'm afraid of?'

'Let's think this through, then.' Her mother's voice dropped. Voice training, thought Laura. 'Suppose you get your scholarship to read English or computer science, what are you going to do then? Take a degree by correspondence, from home? From here? Ashfield Manor Mews? You know very well that you'll go away and stay away like everybody else – in another city, and maybe even in another country. In less than two years' time you could be leaving home anyway! At your age friends are temporary. You might not like it but it's a fact. Friends are temporary, relationships are temporary, school comes to an end, the whole sad muddle of being alive in the first place has a time limit on it, thank God!'

'You sound,' said Laura, 'as if you've reading Bucket McKenzie's T-shirt.'

'And what does that mean?'

'It says, "Life's a bitch, and then you die".'

Up her mother rose, responding to the touch of vulgarity by leaving the room. Then she thought better of it, saying calmly, 'I'm thinking about our future, yours as well as mine. And it's not light years ahead as you seem to think, for tomorrow, let me tell you, has a nasty habit of turning into the here and now ahead of its time.'

'So we're moving then?'

There was no affirmation, merely a stare. Laura finished what she had started. 'You can say what you like. If you want to go to the country and poke at cows with sticks, I'm not going with you. If it's a fight you want, Mother, you can have one. And we'll see who wins!'

She left the room first, and indeed left the house, trembling through all of her body as she carried with her those last words of war the length of Ashfield Avenue.

Eight

When Victoria Clement walked into the school hall with the intention of getting out again as quickly as possible, she found upwards of a hundred other people already gathered there in groups of various sizes, for this was consultation night for the parents of senior pupils and they had come along to hear the stop-press information about their sons and daughters. She herself had three teachers to see, plus a careers master if she thought it would be worthwhile to talk over Laura's options at this stage. First, though, it was a case of smile, nod and move. Avoiding conversation at these functions was an art. She slipped behind the Northern Bank stall to dodge Julie Campbell's parents.

The bank, British Telecom and several other going concerns had erected cute little stalls here and there, each one stocked with leaflets to be handed out. The whole scene was busily informal with just a touch of

70

self-congratulation and hype – the kind of thing the school did rather well. Victoria set off anti-clockwise to escape the absurdly whirling figure of the headmaster, in gown, and bumped into Mr and Mrs Campbell.

While her husband stood by without speaking, fingering a leaflet and dreaming of God knows what, Mrs Campbell said that nobody in this place would give her a straight answer. Julie was thinking of doing Business Studies, but you had to do Accounts. And for Accounts, well, everybody said you needed a certain kind of brain in your head, didn't you? And did Julie have that kind of brain? Nobody would tell her yes or no. Victoria sympathised, and said that she had better find Mr King in case there was a queue.

On that score she need not have worried. Mr King was one of those teachers who announces beforehand that he's giving you eight minutes' worth, the implication being that it's up to you to get value for money before he turfs you out. First he went over Laura's test marks, which placed her, he said, in the second third of a fairly good class. 'Not brilliant but capable,' was the gist of his summing up.

'Works quite well. Has some conceptual difficulties with electromagnetic theory, but this is generally regarded as a difficult part of the course. Have you any questions, Mrs Clement?'

'Well, yes. Would you advise her to take Physics as part of a university degree, or would it be too much of a struggle for her?'

'It helps if one is interested,' he replied, 'and she's not, particularly.'

She found Mr King quite fascinating, because in a way he defied classification in his dull grey suit and his absolute nothing of a green tie. He sat like a statue. Motionless hands protruded from his cuffs. The limpid eyes kept glancing at the disembodied watch lying on the desk and you knew that this one wasn't talking to anyone for more than the allocated eight minutes should you appear before him in your bra and pants. Could he possibly make Physics interesting? Victoria remembered his odd socks, and right now they seemed like his only redeeming feature.

'And how about her behaviour, Mr King?'

'It's not a problem.'

'She's never awkward, then?'

'Never. She lacks interest, that's all.'

As Mr King flicked an uninterested glance at her, Victoria recalled one of Peggy's theories about men. If you put a gold medallion round their necks, ply them with wine and whisk them off to Marbella, you can watch them turn into werewolves at midnight to the sound of castanets and steel guitars. 'Good Lord, Victoria, I don't mean teachers of *Physics*.' Victoria smiled.

'Thank you very much, Mr King. And goodnight.'

It was interesting, she thought on the way home, that only one of Laura's teachers had noticed a change in Laura's behaviour. Mrs Gallagher, the English teacher, declared that, quite frankly, they were now seeing the very best of Laura. This was true both in seminars, where Laura developed and defended her ideas with a nice blend of confidence and humour; and even more in written work, where her interpretations of texts, though sometimes eccentric, were very much her own work and not simply a rehash of other commentators. There was no clearer sign, Mrs Gallagher said, of a maturing mind.

'And I'm sure she's going to make you very proud of her, Mrs Clement.'

'Thank you, Mrs Gallagher. She seems rather taken with Lady Macbeth.'

So the change in Laura – for change there had certainly been – was confined to home and to her mother. Turning into Moat Road with the car more or less on auto-pilot, Victoria tried to shape the small incidents of the last few weeks into a pattern.

Clothes, for instance. Like most of the young ones nowadays, Laura seemed prepared to wear anything of anybody's, the floppier the better, and frequently raided her mother's wardrobe for some acceptable little number. That had not happened recently. Coincidence, perhaps? Or a withdrawal from the negotiation and banter that the process entailed?

Because really, words had been the casualty. As a rule – as Mrs Gallagher had confirmed – Laura had opinions on every subject under the sun. Profound ignorance about a matter had never prevented her from having strong views about it, and yet

74

she now professed herself too bored, almost, to pass the time of day. At no stage had it seemed feasible, and certainly it had not seemed sensible, to talk to her about moving house. Since it takes two to talk, Victoria had collaborated in the creation of a limbo of silence wherein everything was too important or too trivial to mention.

It was a huff, of course, she thought as she closed the garage door. You're not doing what I want you to do, so I'll punish you. There will be sanctions. Children discovered that a huff was a thing of great power even before they went to school. 'If you don't do what I want you to do I'll shout and scream and hate you.' It was, perhaps, their earliest weapon, and they carried it into the street with them: 'If you don't do what I want you to do I'll not be your friend.' Somewhat uneasily, Victoria remembered that the common-or-garden huff was used by adults too. 'If you don't do what I want you to do I'll make you suffer, somehow.' It was a strategy people used from the cradle to the grave.

Within the house one light only burned, the one they jokingly referred to as their anti-burglar device, so Laura was still out with her new friend Stephen. And there, of course, was another complication. It was so easy, at that age, to imagine that a boyfriend was the most precious thing you could or would ever have . . .

Later that evening, after a short burst of ironing, she took some clothes up to Laura's room and left them on the bed for her. There on the dressing table she encountered an old photograph of Bob that she hadn't seen for years. It showed him with a fish, beaming, full of himself! She remembered that lough shore near Ballynahinch, she remembered the day, and she remembered the landing of the great fish, a thrashing pike. The photograph was propped up against Teddy.

And then, as if caught herself on a glittering lure, she lingered to notice other things – the candle she and Laura had brought back from Edinburgh; the fan, damaged that summer's day by a foolish swipe at a wasp; a black and white still from an old movie starring Steve McQueen; the diary, lying closed. By this naming of objects Victoria found herself charting her daughter's progress through time to the here and now. At one end of the continuum she, Victoria, had been at the heart of everything with Teddy and the toys; at the other . . . well, the diary was, and must remain, a closed book to her for ever.

Nostalgia! It was self-indulgent. Worse. It was treacherous.

Downstairs, she phoned Jim.

'How are things?' he asked her.

'What can I say? It's quite rough at this end, really. There's no getting through to her, Jim, but then again, I haven't really tried because . . . Well, it's bad practice to give in to this sort of thing, I just know deep down it is. I've never done it before. Did I tell you she has a boyfriend?'

'Ah, but she's young,' he said.

'And when I was like her, Jim, I couldn't keep my feet on the ground if a certain somebody smiled at me. I see him yet the odd time in Royal Avenue!'

She heard him chuckle. 'What's he like?'

'Forty. Ordinary. Like me.'

'Do you want me to speak to her, Vicky?'

'No, no.' The thought of the two of them meeting was just too bizarre to dwell on. 'It wouldn't help, not now. And it hasn't been too long, really. We'll just have to be patient, Jim. Wait and see what happens.'

Nine

After school they came down the hill, all ears, listening to the Margaret Lapsley show.

Margaret walked in the middle, flanked by Julie and Laura, both of whom inclined their heads slightly inwards in an effort to hear every word of what Margaret had to say about her contacts with people beyond the grave. And it was riveting stuff, by no means for the faint-hearted. Last night Margaret and her cronies had been in touch with a Chicago newspaper boy who had been kicked in the head by a brewer's horse in the 1930s.

'What did he want to talk to you lot for?' Julie inquired.

'He was lost,' said Margaret. ' "Lost" in the astral sense,' she hastened to explain – 'searching for serenity.'

'You couldn't plug into Macbeth?' suggested Julie. 'Might give us a few tips for the exams.'

'It's not like calling people up on the phone, Julie! And anyway, Macbeth's in a book.'

Laura, appraising her friend Margaret with carefully timed sidelong glances, half expected to see her crackling with psychic energy.

'But it's all pressure and friction, Margaret,' she said. 'Everybody has a finger on the glass – the pressure can't remain equal on the rim and so the glass is bound to move. It's physics. And when you're dead, that's it.'

These observations were parried with gentle calm and even pity as Margaret went on to mention a member of the Russian royal family who would only say, 'My jewels, my jewels,' and sometimes, she said, the glass shook on the table and you had to quit. 'Why?' breathed Julie. Because an evil spirit had hijacked the astral contact lines and was trying to break through to real time. It was a form of nonsense so enthralling that none of them noticed the grey car pulling up at the kerb alongside.

'Is that fool of a car honking its hooter at us or somebody else?' Julie muttered bullishly.

80

It was Stephen. Laura spotted the R-plate on the windscreen as he opened the door with the kind of beam on his face that sells toothpaste.

'Would you like a lift?'

'Who's a clever boy then!' shrieked Julie.

'Will you get in, I'm holding up the traffic.'

Julie brazenly occupied the front seat beside him and cried, 'Home, James! Take us to Laura's house for coffee. He can come, can't he, Laura?'

'If he knows the way.'

The back seat was better, anyway – she could plainly see his eyes enclosed within the rim of the driving mirror. When she winked, he winked back.

'Indicate, mirror, move off, that's how it's done. Dead easy.' Julie grabbed for a seat belt, and he said, 'Are you nervous, or something?'

'Look, you, somebody told me people often have accidents just after their test because they're so cocky and full of themselves, so watch it. I don't want to end up talking to Margaret Lapsley through a glass tumbler.'

'I'm not just after my test, I've been driving since lunchtime. Singing "American Pie." '

'Did you get the one with the moustache?' Laura leaned forward to ask.

'Never noticed.'

'He never noticed!' declared Julie. 'How could you miss the moustache on somebody's face?'

'You never look them in the eye. It's just like dogs, if you look them in the eye they think you're putting up a challenge to them.'

'Such twaddle! You know Donna Swain? Hers had a moustache and she nearly kissed him when he said she'd passed.'

'She'd kiss anything,' Stephen said. 'You should have seen my emergency stop. Perfection! Why are you looking so glum, Laura?'

'Fear. I'll never do it, honestly, I'll be the first one in the form to fail it.'

'Wrong, Pinky failed his but he never let on. And guess what Pinky didn't have.'

'Wheels on his car?' Julie said.

'Bucket's lucky L-plates.' Another wink in the driving mirror. 'And here we are at

Ashfield Manor Mews.'

In the end Stephen decided that he wouldn't come in for coffee, preferring, as he put it, to drive round the town and be seen by all the walking peasants. Laura whispered, 'You're great!' into his ear before he drove away, then turned to find Julie regarding her suspiciously.

'He stopped that car right at the very house you live in, Laura.'

'Hmm.' She didn't tell, either, about the gift of L-plates or the tenpin bowling. 'I wouldn't put it past him to know my phone number and all. Hold this while I dig out my key.'

'What is it?'

'A poster. Miss Watson let me paint it during private study this afternoon. I used to be good at Art, you may remember.'

But Art, said Mother, who claimed to have experience of this shifting world, Art would not necessarily pay the bills in the silicone days ahead – best to choose a gilt-edged subject, Laura. Think small, think micro-chip. She smoothed out the painting for Julie to admire.

'Well, it's very yellow, isn't it? Like

83

thingummy who sliced off his ear.'

'It's the front of our house, dope.'

'Oh yeah. You'd think the house had only one eye the way it's squinting through those trees.'

'Laburnums, Julie. Exactly how Mother likes to see them in the spring. Like all the best Art, this takes over where words fail – it is a representation of the undefinable.'

'The what?'

'Something vague and mysterious with deep roots that touch everything. You don't put lemon-coloured fronds into words or you ordinarify them, any fool knows that. Daddy planted them. I'll stick it up on my wall where it can't be missed.'

'Right, the penny has dropped, you're into psychological warfare. How are things between you, by the way?'

How indeed, Laura found herself wondering. 'Worse.'

Probably the darkest thing was that they had no fun any more, humour had gone out the window. How could you risk a smile when it might be interpreted as a sign of weakness?

But no, the lack of humour was not quite

the worst thing. The worst thing was that Laura had come to appreciate how little she understood about her mother. Just by sitting where she sat, by looking as she looked, by doing what she did and by being what she was, her mother's cold, daunting, implacable presence filled the house with a hostility so calm that it almost seemed to be a rare form of serenity. The shock had come when Laura realised that it was not a matter of her mother having banished her 'real' self somewhere else for the time being, this was not an act. The coldness was in her, *was* her. Had always been her? I know what it feels like, she thought, to be this slug that turned.

How are things between you? Julie's question was not difficult to answer, but suddenly she found an answer difficult to express aloud. She could only describe a bleakness which she, too, had helped to fashion, and this felt like a failure. She simply shrugged her shoulders and said again, 'Things are worse.'

'I suppose she's just trying to be happy,' Julie mused. 'It's a pity he wouldn't come and live with you here.'

'Oh, I suggested that long ago.'

'And?'

'No.'

Almost amused, Mother had been. How could you expect a man to sell his land and his animals, Laura! In other words *he* couldn't leave a bunch of pigs, but she, Laura, was supposed to give up all her human friends with a wave and a cheerio.

'Oh well, never mind, look what I've got for you,' said Julie, miraculously producing from nowhere the grottiest pair of L-plates ever seen. She dangled them from her ears, and the hooting began.

'How did you get them!'

'Favours.'

'Julie!'

'Well, he needed a homework to copy so I said, what's in it for me and he said you can have my luscious fruity body or my lucky L-plates. I thought it over for about two seconds and took the L-plates. Aren't they priceless? I didn't know plastic wore away.'

The doorbell sounded. Possibly Mother, but unlikely – it was practically inconceivable that she could lose her key.

Glancing through the side window in the lounge, Laura saw a woman with a briefcase on the doorstep, yet another smart business lady in the makings of a uniform. Blue and yellow scarf at the throat, matching slate-blue skirt. A touch of yellow, even, in the shoes.

She opened the door.

'Good afternoon. I'm looking for Mrs Victoria Clement. I represent the estate agent named on this card. I like your garden. Very much so.'

'She's not in yet,' said Laura, scanning the card in her hand. The Belltower Company. Auctioneers, estate agents, valuers.

'Oh dear, that's a pity. I'm Rosemary Gordon, by the way. And we did actually arrange this time of day because it was convenient for us both.'

'Probably the traffic's bad,' said Laura, returning the card, which featured a little blue bell on a yellow background.

'Indeed, I know what it's like!' Rosemary Gordon smiled. She was about twenty-six, Laura surmised; pretty, petite, good teeth and awfully nice with the public. 'Preserve us from Shaftesbury Square in the rush hour! Could I possibly come in anyway and look over the house? We could always advise your mum of our findings by phone.'

'Why do you want to look at the house?'

'To value it.'

'You mean – what it's worth?'

'Well, we have to put a price on the property before it goes on the market, obviously.'

Laura said, as she steadied the moving door, 'Sell it, you mean?'

'If your mother proceeds, yes. But this is only a preliminary . . .'

'Would you excuse me for a minute, please, I've got milk on the cooker.'

Laura hared back to the kitchen, where she closed the door with an almighty thump. Julie observed her slight breathlessness with curiosity.

'What's up?'

'An estate agent.'

'Well, thank God. I thought you'd clapped eyes on a Lapsley ghost.'

'She wants to put a price on the house!'

What to say? Up until this moment they had been talking ifs and buts about moving house and now the reality had arrived on the doorstep, it even had a name.

'I'll tell her the place is a mess.'

'Laura, that won't matter. All she wants to know is how many rooms have you got and is there fungus on the walls. If you leave her out there much longer she'll turn into a milkbottle.'

'You're a big help, Julie,' she said, closing her eyes, feeling her pulse throbbing away at various points of her body. But at this moment and in this house the authority was hers and no way was Miss Gordon, that stranger, getting in.

She returned to the door. 'I'm sorry about that.'

'It's quite all right, really.'

'I'm afraid I can't let you in, though. You might be a con man. Or a con person if you prefer.'

'I beg your pardon?'

Only the innocent blush. 'You know what I mean,' Laura said easily, 'they are operating in this area at the moment and Mum says I'm to be extra careful about who I let into the house. We're getting a burglar alarm soon.'

Up came the briefcase to balance on a

horizontal thigh. 'But that is ridiculous. I have these with me – I'll show you. Headed notepaper with the Belltower logo, a measuring tape, calculator . . .'

'Anyone might have those,' Laura gravely pointed out, 'and I don't want to talk about this any more, so please go away.'

She closed the door on Rosemary Gordon and her briefcase, then darted into the lounge, where Julie already peeked through a split in the velvet curtains like a born spy.

'She's getting into her car now. Hey, your front gate sure knows it's been closed, Laura. I bet that's the first time anybody ever called her a con person!' Julie paused for a convulsive snigger. 'Anyway, what did she look like? Twitchy?'

'Hypnotised.' Laura cast herself on to the sofa. 'My legs, they're like jelly. The woman must think I'm a raving loony but it was the only thing I could think of and what's she going to *say*? I'll get crucified!"

'You mean – Mother?'

'Too right, I mean Mother.'

'Well, maybe she is a crook for all we know. People pose as anything these days to get their filthy hands on a few quids' worth of video recorder.'

'Julie, I saw her, she was wearing a linen suit with a matching thing at the neck, exactly the sort of outfit Mother wears to the office – not to mention that case full of gadgets. She was the real thing, don't let's kid ourselves.'

'That's all right, then. You did the right thing, you sent her packing.'

Until the next time. This had been one small skirmish, there would be plenty more. Was there really any doubt about who would be doing the packing?

Ten

On Saturday morning she met Jim for coffee at a road-house they liked in the country. It was handy for him on that side of town, and she enjoyed driving between hedges for a change, travelling by way of Comber. He was anxious to talk to her about Laura.

But he didn't understand what was happening, not really. Perhaps it wasn't surprising that Jim couldn't get his mind round the problem, Victoria reflected, for he had not seen fit to get married in spite of robust good looks, and consequently had no children of his own to colour his ideas on how to deal with them. Rather like Peggy, in fact, although Peggy at least had a sister whose second son had driven the family to distraction when he 'got religion'. (Or when religion got him, as Peggy put it dryly.) Jim didn't even have that kind of vicarious experience to rely on. He was in favour of a military solution. Send in the marines.

So it was her task this morning to put him wise, to explain how you could say no more than 'pass the toast' in a whole day; to explain how you could talk and talk the next day until everything was said and nothing was settled. It was obvious after ten minutes that he grew tired of hearing all this, that he wanted to talk of other, sweeter things; but he listened. And from the manner of his listening – tight-lipped, frown lines deep under the sandy fringe – Victoria knew that he was still feeling gung-ho.

So she mentioned the photographs, and how Laura had taken down all the posters from the walls of her room – gone were Steve McQueen and some awful hollow-faced modern pop creature – to replace them with photographs of everyone she knew, including Bucket McKenzie.

'Bucket?'

Don't ask, she said, smiling, and went on to establish the importance of the photographs. Each face had a large X under it to indicate that she, Victoria – Mother – was eliminating it, causing it to cease to exist. It was the destruction of an emotional landscape, hence the picture on the wall from a Sunday magazine.

'What picture?'

A ruined rainforest, she told him, spelling out the grand allusion. Another example of wilful destruction. And he began to shake his head. He was seeing the problem, the size of the problem.

Over a second cup of coffee she told him about Sniff the teddy bear. Strangely enough Victoria couldn't recall why it had such a peculiar name, although she guessed that it had something to do with some funny little thing Laura used to say when she was learning to talk. Anyway, the name wasn't important. The point was that Laura had made a placard for Teddy.

'A placard? To hold, you mean?'

'To hold,' she said. There sat Sniff on the pine dressing table, holding up a triangular flag with three words written on it: Teddy Says No.

For the first time Victoria saw the fear in his eyes. He said a single, profane word which sounded out of character.

'Victoria, let me speak to her.'

'And say what?'

'I don't know what. The truth! I love you and I'd care for her and I'd see that she wanted for nothing. Money-wise she'd be better off.'

Victoria nodded. And then, she said, there was the painting of the laburnums, an uncannily skilful creation in all honesty, and warm – warm the way a child's first drawing of a square house is warm. A reminder that Mother had urged her to develop her intelligence rather than her talent. The medium was messenger and message.

'Bob planted the trees, you understand.'

'Very subtle!' he said brutally. She couldn't figure out whether he intended this as sarcasm.

'If you talk to her, Jim, it might make things worse. I'm convinced she must be living on her nerves the same as me.'

His temper reared up. 'Doesn't she think you deserve a break? It's *self* all the time, isn't it, that's what it boils down to. I'd tell her you don't deserve this, Vicky, that's what I'd tell her.'

'Maybe so. There's something I found out years ago, Jim. Whoever or whatever is running things up there doesn't have a complaints department.'

It was almost a relief when, coming home, she bumped into Peggy in the shopping complex at Sprucefield. After talking to Jim, conversation with Peggy felt like getting on a bus: one was simply whisked along without having to think.

'I don't care what anybody says, Victoria, these supermarket places have no soul, listen to that awful piped music. Speaking of which, that man George Adams says he can't understand why people want Gilbert and Sullivan when they could have Offenbach instead. Well, you know what I think of Offenbach. George Adams, I said, this is the North of Ireland and not Gay Paree, Offenbach is just an excuse for putting half-naked people on the stage. Well may you laugh, Victoria, but you only have to think of *Orpheus* or *La Belle Hélène*. Mind that coleslaw.'

Victoria, backing away in fits, had almost upended a splendid display of salads. 'And what did he say, Peggy?'

'What could he say, all he did was

swallow his tea rather quickly so I assume we've heard the last of *that* nonsense. Now. I want you to tell me that everything is sorted out and you're as happy as a cricket. Because it could be worse, you know. You've heard me talk about my sister Marion in Cookstown? Her second boy? Anyway, Holy War has broken out. Church on Sundays isn't good enough for him, he wants to drag them out on Wednesday nights as well. And as for drink, well, alcohol is the devil's blood, so you can think about that the next time you pour yourself a dry martini. Marion says it's like living with an alien. I think it's all a phase they go through, Victoria – Laura's going to be fine.'

Fanaticism, she thought in the car, has many forms, many strategies. She remembered, too, the flash of fear she'd seen that day in Jim's eyes – a fear that she wouldn't be strong enough, that she would be the one to back down. Was he wiser than she knew? Didn't the fact that she hadn't yet tackled Laura about Rosemary Gordon, her business friend from the Belltower Company, imply a certain lack of resolve?

97

She would do so at tea.

'I see you have managed to acquire three sets of L-plates for the car, Laura. However did you manage that?'

'One set I bought, the second set Stephen gave me and the grotty ones are Bucket McKenzie's.'

'Grotty is right.'

'They're supposed to be lucky. Nobody has ever failed their test with those plates on the car, according to Bucket.'

There was something about that name 'Bucket' that made Victoria wince. 'Well, he sounds like a fool. When it comes to the driving test one makes one's own luck, as you'll find out.' And she paused, experiencing a sensation of taking them both into a blind tunnel. '*If* there's a driving test at all, I should add.'

'What do you mean *if*?'

'I think you probably know what I mean. I'm talking about you learning to drive and I wonder why I should bother.'

Laura flicked a glance at her. 'No problem. Let me take lessons if you don't want to bother teaching me yourself.'

It was the 'no problem' which cut most deeply. That casual little remark rejected her entirely. Nothing you do, Mother, nothing you say can set up an obstacle I can't get round.

'It really is wonderful to see how you take everything in your stride, Laura, because you take everything for granted. Your coldness towards me at the present time and your stubborn behaviour are making me suffer, frankly. I ask myself why I should fork out all the money it's going to take to get you on the road if it's all 'no problem'? I'm talking about driving lessons, you understand, and a whole lot more besides. I'm talking about wear and tear, clutch cables, tyres, licence fees, test fees, not to mention the cost of insuring my car for you to drive. Or the petrol. Why, Laura?' And she waited. 'Well?'

'Because you're my mother, because you brought me into the world and I can't get out of it, is that a good enough reason?'

'It's pathetic. It's what every self-absorbed teenager manages to say to her parents sooner or later and it literally reeks of unoriginality. The estate agent called at this house recently and you refused to let her in. Perhaps you'd like to explain that, too.'

Laura put on a pose of profound indifference, but the creeping blush betrayed her. 'You didn't tell me she was coming that day so how was I supposed to know who she was?'

'Oh yes, I heard, you practically accused that woman – who is an acquaintance of mine, incidentally – of being a house-to-house con artist! It wasn't even an official visit, she was doing me a favour.'

Then, suddenly, there came a wail, a distortion of speech. 'You've no right to sell this house!'

'I have every right, it's my house.'

'Ours! I live here too, you know.'

Victoria Clement watched, appalled. The change coming over her daughter now was almost chemical. After weeks, ice turns to magma and tears.

'Daddy would want me to be here and I'll say it's got dry rot and I'll say it's got woodworm when all the buyers come in here and start tramping over everything that's *mine*.'

Victoria lowered herself until she met one

of the hard dining chairs. 'Oh God.'

'And you can keep your money because I've got legs and I'll walk, I'll get the bus and I don't care if I never learn to drive your precious car. And then . . . then you'll really have me, won't you? I won't even be a lodger when you go to Bangor, will I? I'll be nothing but a bloody prisoner!'

Then she wheeled around and left the room, needing no reply, and getting none.

Victoria Clement remained to gaze inertly at the small portions of mixed cheeses she'd bought earlier in the day: Brie, Danish Blue, Feta. A nose of French bread lay there, too. Curiously, her head was thumping, not her heart. After a moment she turned on the radio simply to hear someone talking.

Eleven

That evening when Stephen called, Laura said that she didn't want to go anywhere in particular – unless he had plans – she just wanted to go. Oh, anywhere quiet, she said, there'd been a row with Mother, the full works. When he looked at her in a thinking sort of way she suddenly doubted whether she was up to the idle chatter that makes people comfortable with one another. But she smiled and fetched her coat.

In the car he said, 'I hope it wasn't about me.'

'What?'

'The argument you had with your mother.'

'Stephen, I don't want to spoil your happiness but you didn't even get a mention.'

'Story of my life.'

Then she suddenly grinned, recalling one of the lighter moments of recent days. 'Anyway, you're OK. I told her you said she was so like my sister we could advertise soap.'

'I didn't say that!'

'Julie never tells a lie, Stephen.'

'But she doesn't half exaggerate!'

They continued to talk about Julie behind her back; about school; the *Highway Code*; his family. One of his sisters was getting married and bullying him into being an usher at the wedding. ('What does it even *mean*, how do you *ush*?') Eventually they parked on a shore of Lough Neagh, where Laura said how much she would like to paint the last gleam of light lying on the water and among the rushes.

'Not many people windsurfing, all the same,' he said.

'Would you? The clocks go back in three weeks. It must be freezing out there.'

'Nice, though. I bring all my girlfriends here.'

She duly walloped him; and when they settled, an arm moved round her shoulder like a long feather with legs on it. 'Do you want some music?'

'Yes. Go on then, sing!' She laughed and snuggled into the arm as if burrowing for heat. 'This is what I want. I could stay like this forever if it wasn't for this poky-up gearstick between us.'

'You can't get gearstickless cars, Laura.'

'Can't you, Stephen?'

Did her mother sit somewhere like this? Love's young dream? It occurred to her that no one in the world knew where she was at this moment except Stephen – there was no special place where she was meant to be, where they could reach her; and how rare that was! All her life she'd had a cowbell round her neck to make known her whereabouts. Her time had never been her own, had it? Someone doled time out to her in rations, there had never been any choice in how to use it if you excluded going to the loo. So much for freedom!

'It must be nice,' she said, 'to be able to get into the car and just go.'

'It would be nice if you didn't have to fork out for the petrol.'

'Where would you go?'

'Alpha Centauri. But I'd need a space-ship.'

Laura prised herself upright to face him in the gloom. 'How much would it cost to drive to a planet called Bangor?'

'And back again? I'd say easily the guts of a fiver's worth.'

'Would you take me there tomorrow if I pay for the petrol?'

'I didn't mean . . .'

'I'd pay,' said Laura. 'It would only be fair. And I'd like Julie to come too. Would you mind?'

'I don't mind. Why Bangor?'

'I've to see somebody there.'

And you wouldn't easily guess who, she thought. My next daddy.

As had so often been the case at recent times, they had a peculiar little conversation at breakfast, for it was tinted with a touch of melancholy. Laura said she didn't see the point of going to the harvest service when a majority of the world's babies died of starvation, while her mother, already dressed in a grey suit argued that, on the whole, the clergy were nice humble people who deserved some of one's loyalty in an age which adored wealth, power and aggressive leadership. 'Belief has little to do with it, it's a cultural activity, Laura. Goodbye.'

'I'll be out for lunch. Stephen, Julie and me are going for a drive.'

A nod, and Mother went off to the harvest service alone.

'Haven't been down in this part of the world for donkeys! Dad and me used to come all the time, you know, when I was a kid. Fishing. We used to catch mackerel off Orlock Head. One day I got twenty-seven fish in half an hour using the spinner. It was magic. The last Saturday in August, it was.'

Stephen spoke above the noise of the engine and Radio One. Julie responded from the back seat.

'That's nearly a fish a minute. I don't believe mackerel are that stupid, do you, Laura?'

'I've never tasted them,' Laura said vaguely.

She found it more soothing to watch the roadside skimming by than to pay attention to what was being shouted backwards and forwards in the car, and indeed there were times when she didn't hear them at all, for there were other voices to be listened to, the ones inside her head: little cameos of past conversations and full-scale rehearsals of conversations to come. What would she say to Jim Mulholland, for example?

'Right! So we're talking here about the wholesale slaughter of innocent wee fish. I hope you come back as a mackerel in your next life, Stevie Kennedy, and get a dirty great hook in your top lip!'

'No chance, I'll be a shark – one long awesome streak of death.'

'You hear that, Laura? He's going to be one long awesome streak of death. *Jaws the Eighth* starring Stevie Kennedy.'

'Turn left past this gate.'

So they had passed Dunne's Lane and the farm with the three rust-coloured byres and were now in the territory where Granny Stirling knitted out her days. What was she doing here? To say to Jim Mulholland yes, root me up, cart me off and start me all over again? Had she come to surrender after five weeks of drawing on a well of anger she hadn't even known was there?

But the well was empty, almost. The hours of the week that were hers no longer existed, the feud had taken over. She opened a book and got to the bottom of a page, read every line but every word was meaningless because she'd been thinking of what Mother said last or what she should do next. Glancing sideways at Stephen, who was still rabbiting on about fish, she wondered dispassionately how long their relationship would last. What would make him drive the guts of a fiver's worth when the girl next door was available? Presumably even love could be significantly affected by market forces.

Harbinsons' house. They used to have a pony and a curtain that pulled across the front door to save it from the sun. The curtain had been striped like the cloth on a deck chair. In there, for the first and last time in her life, years ago, she'd actually used a croquet mallet.

'Turn left again, Stephen.'

'What does your mum drive, Laura?' he asked.

'A Fiat.'

'Do you like it?'

'I don't like it or not like it, it's just a car. The road gets narrower round this bend.'

A tractor loomed up in front of them – fetching a squeal out of Julie, for it seemed to fill the road – and forced Stephen to stop with the wheel of the car resting on the crest of a ditch.

'Narrow is right! Where are we, anyway?'

'If it's not the back of beyond it's the front!' cried Julie. 'How do people live here? I'd be up to a hundred every time the wind blew.'

They passed Granny Stirling's converted cottage on the right. Thinking back, Laura seemed to remember that Jim Mulholland had helped her to extend the kitchen.

'Stop at the bottom of this hill. There's a gateway with white pillars just past the beech trees. You can see the house from the road.'

'That pebble-dashed place?' Stephen sounded impressed. 'It's a fine big house, all the same.'

'If you don't mind looking out at tin barns and if you don't mind the smell of cow dung.'

'I thought you said he keeps pigs?' said Julie.

'Same difference. Wait for me here, Stephen. I wouldn't think I'll be long.'

With the turning off of the car's engine they were enclosed within a quiet that grew more and more formidable as the seconds went by. As Laura opened the door, Julie said, 'All right, Laura, we're here, what do you say we just go home again?'

'What was the point in coming, then?'

'OK, what are you going to say to him? If he's in at all, that is. I mean, I know it's none of my business really, fair enough, but if you waltz up there and find yourself face to face in the middle of the farmyard absolutely *wordless*, what'll you do? Like . . . I'd just conk out, let me tell you. Is it wise?'

Laura said, 'I don't know what's wise and what isn't,' and closed the door from the outside.

Left alone in the car with Stephen, Julie watched him fiddle with the knob of the radio until she could stand the crackling and the snatches of foreign voices no longer.

'Will you cut that out? Laura's in an awful state about all this and you sit there trying to get Radio Honolulu. Did she tell you about it?'

He nodded. 'Last night.'

'I hope it wasn't you put her up to this jaunt, Stevie Kennedy.'

'Nope. I said if it was me I'd have to go, like it or lump it.'

'Which is easy to say when nobody's dragging you out here to live. *Look* at the place – it would be like a jail sentence.'

And he did glance, casually, through the windscreen at the far horizon. Like someone humouring an idiot, Julie thought. 'Well?'

'I reckon I could live just about anywhere with the right person.'

'Oooh! Anybody in mind for this love nest in the wilderness?'

'I think you're a bit upset, too,' Stephen said.

Julie glared at a berry-rich hawthorn hedge through the side window, a little chastened by his reply, but convinced, all the same, of the pointlessness of talking to him. He hadn't the wit to see that Laura didn't have the right person. Her mother did.

She saw Laura disappear round the far end of a row of those goldy-coloured trees.

Approaching the end of Mulholland's wide, dark lane, Laura found herself presented with a choice of routes: whether to continue down the lane, which now became brown and guttery as the rain mixed with farmyard juices, or to make directly for the front door through a gate in the walled garden. The gate seemed marginally less intimidating.

Until she ventured through it and discovered trees that would have dwarfed an entire garden in Ashfield Manor Mews. The house, close up, seemed more ornate because of the fiddly bits of roof that swept down and surrounded two of the upper-storey windows. A species of flame-coloured ivy had a free run of the entire front wall; and yes, it was impressive. Here was a house and garden that went back for generations. Laura could easily imagine little Victoria Stirling swinging over there on a strung-up rubber tyre.

But no one answered the door. She walked along the front of the house (Victorian conservatory-to-be?) and through yet another gate into the original lane. Crossing this boundary between house and farm, she came upon an open barn as big as a church and just as empty. A big spiky machine lay at the entrance like an evil relic from a medieval torture chamber and beyond, a honey-coloured stairway of straw bales disappeared into the gloom of the roof. After two more steps she brought to life a brute of a dog which was thankfully tethered to a chain. Unable to reach her and eat her, the beast lapsed into a fit of howling misery.

Jim Mulholland appeared. 'Mo! Here to me, Mo. Come by and be still!' A glance at Laura, then, 'You'll be all right, he's more bark than . . .'

He recognised her. You could see the moment of recognition taking instant effect, but not for long. 'Easy, Mo. There now. Laura Clement. It's a while since I've seen you. It must be . . . Well, it's a fair wee while.'

And he knocked back his cap to show a roll of springy hair. He had flame-coloured ears to match the ivy.

'Nearly two years, actually,' Laura said.

'It would be all of that, yes.'

'New Year's Eve at Granny Stirling's.'

'There y'are, now. Well, I want you to

113

know that you're welcome. You're like your mother. You've grown up very like your mother.'

'Have I.'

The tone suggested that she was not to be drawn into an exchange of dull-edged pleasantries. Whatever kind of communication they were about to have – and still she did not know – it would not be classed as ordinary.

'Would you come inside?'

'No, thank you.'

'It's starting to rain.'

'I'm not here to beg,' she said, 'I'm not here to ask you to change your mind if that's what you're thinking.'

With a slow hand he continued to stroke the whining dog. 'You won't change my mind. Step into the barn, then, out of the wet.'

'I don't like the smell of pigs.'

'You don't need to like the smell of pigs to stand out of the rain, but mind yourself on the prongs of that raker. I'll let loose the dog or he'll not settle. His name's Mo.'

She found herself not caring what its name was so long as it didn't jump up on her; but the beast ran off on a sniffing expedition. The rain began to ping heavily on the tin roof, making her look up.

'Does Vicky – your mother – does she know you're here?'

'Will you want me to change my name?' she said.

'Your name?'

'To Mulholland. Will I stay as Laura Clement or will I have to become Laura Mulholland?'

'You're Bob's daughter down to the genes and chromosomes, we both know nothing will ever change that, so does a name matter?'

'It matters to me.'

'And you came all the way down here,' he said evenly, 'to tell me that you're not changing your name?'

'All the way is right. And the answer is no, that's not why I came.'

She conceded nothing to his steady gaze, even though she looked away first to focus on a break in the far clouds above the low roof of the pig house.

'I'm glad you came,' he was saying. 'Your mum has been through a lot recently,

I'm sure of that. You too, probably. We've done a lot of talking . . .'

'That doesn't surprise me, she discusses these things with everybody except me.'

'From what I hear,' he said sharply, 'you're anything but easy to talk to.'

'Depends on who's doing the talking, doesn't it?'

'Well now, I'm not quite sure what that means, if it means anything at all. Anyway, of course you'll retain the name of your natural father.'

'Gee, thanks.'

'Don't mention it. You should understand that I'm not begging, either.'

It was almost – it felt like – a threat. She sensed that he could be as flinty and crude as she in these word games, cry na-na-na in the street with her or meet reason with reason if that was what she chose; and at this moment he was waiting for her to speak again as the rain swirled by the open mouth of the barn.

'What else have you discussed, then? Where will I live? In the attic?' Or the kennel, she felt like saying. The dog had returned for more fondling.

'If you really wanted an answer to that question you would come in and see the house.'

'And school? How do you expect me to get to school from here in the mornings? My new school!' A flash of impatience showed in his face. 'Or is that too much of a detail for anybody to worry about but me, because *I'm* the one who'll have to leave the house at seven and get back home again at *six*.'

'Look, it would surely be best if your mother was here and we could talk over these things together?'

'And she's too old to have children, you know. Or is that another fiddly detail that nobody cares about?'

Up until this moment Jim Mulholland had been regarding her quite calmly, dividing his attention more or less evenly between her and the wandering creature Mo; but now he became still, as if to listen to a more distant sound, and he stared at the pebble-dashed gable wall in which some small stones glistened like sequins after the rain.

'Oh, good God,' he said.

'Well it's true! I saw a programme about it, they could be born with something wrong with them.'

'Look, I don't want to listen to this. *You're* here to do damage.'

'And you're one to talk.'

He flung out a hand, banishing her and all she had to say. 'Go on home! You're here to hurt, and hurting's always easy, isn't it? The easy option! You don't even have to take aim, dammit, all you young ones have to do is open your mouths and you do more harm than you can ever dream about. Honest to God, you know nothing, you can't see from here to there, everything nice and simple, black and white, I'm number one and the devil take the hindmost! Get away home!'

The dog, too, gave vent to a howl of abuse.

'I'm going,' Laura said, unnerved.

'Come on, Mo. Easy, boy, easy.'

Away he marched, legs like scissor blades crossing.

'And this won't ever be my home!' she flung after him down the empty yard.

The rain was in her face. Laura, her body vibrating still from the residue of unexpended energy, left without a backward glance. Later she would remember every word she'd said and should have said, but for now such clarity was beyond her and she only knew for certain what her feelings were.

She hated Jim Mulholland. That authentic discovery came into her mind and blood-stream with the lightness of exhilaration. And yet she came to a halt as she walked through the tunnel of trees, and stood quite still for some time.

Over there was the big house, rippling. Waiting, even, among trees that would dwarf laburnums. On this side a gathering of contented black and white cows in a sheltered hollow. And all around leaves trickled off the trees in the moist wind. She was seeing her mother's lost, familiar world on a harvest Sunday – back there was the man she said she loved. And what, then, if she, Laura, were to tap into the well of hate she felt within? She knew it would be a wrong thing to do, unambiguously wrong, as stealing is wrong, or murder. It would be to choose darkness.

Twelve

'Jim, I'll see you in an hour at Mother's. And I'm so sorry about this. Apart from anything else I can't get over her sheer bad manners!'

'Ah, well now,' his voice said, 'I have to say that I wasn't the height of diplomacy myself.'

'In an hour.'

Victoria, reversing with abandon into the Mews, belatedly began to wonder whether panic had not gripped her with something of its manic force. Why was she going down there? It must be to see Jim. Because when damage has been done, after all, you want to reach out, touch and heal, especially when you feel, however irrationally, that the guilt is partly yours. Or maybe she didn't trust herself just to sit and wait and be alone with her daughter when she came home. Driving was an activity.

But the madness of her going there! And the horror of what she had said. Jim, most likely, hadn't told her the half of it. Had she taken the bus? Where was she now? At Granny Stirling's? Victoria's heart sank at the thought of Mother, who would have wise and wondrous things to say about something that was beyond her understanding. 'Does the child know you love her, Vicky?' had been last Friday's gem of a question. 'I just think that young ones can take harder knocks if they know people are dying about them.'

It had been said quietly, but the implied judgement on her seventeen years of child-rearing had taken Victoria's breath away. Does the child know you love her!

Flabby, banal, senseless question! Not even a question – a line from a simpering country song! She had no particular proofs to offer – didn't the whole hard, single-handed struggle speak for itself, day after day of proofs in action, proofs so drab and boring and obvious that they were utterly forgettable, stories read, meals made, lifts in cars, nights with teeth, burying dead rabbits, pinning up drawings, clothes pressed, the list was endless, that list they gave you when they brought you the precious bundle in the first place. Does the child know you love her!

But what she did *not* believe, was that parents should sacrifice bits of themselves to keep the children happy. It didn't work and it was not her style.

And now with a simple stroke Laura had gathered in everyone who could claim a right to speak in this sorry mess, and Laura's mother found herself wondering whether it was the simplicity of wickedness or despair. Either way, same disaster. Victoria slowed down, for she had been driving like hell along wet and quiet Sunday roads. Wouldn't it be just like the thing if she put the car over the ditch! For several hundred metres she constructed a scenario, the centrepiece of which was her own funeral.

Not that she would be surprised if something unspeakable lay ahead, for she had lately been in that frame of mind where premonitions and fears loom large during the housework. Only last week Laura had run away and ended up a waif on the streets of London in the time it took her mother to iron a blouse.

In the narrow road she parked tight against Granny Stirling's front rail – close enough for some giant ears of rhubarb to tickle the car door. Extraordinary rhubarb. Jim had put in three crowns only last August and the stuff had taken off so beautifully that it had become one of life's small talking points. Hardly today, though. It would be neglected today. Does the rhubarb know you love it, Mother?

The front door lay wide open to the world. 'Are you there, Mummy?'

She appeared from the depths of the house, dumpy-looking in the eternal pinny.

'Vicky! What are you doing here the day?'

A plastic pinny, advertising an aristocratic but defunct line of soap. The arms were bare and plump in the way that her cheeks and fingers were plump; indeed, her wedding ring seemed so tight that one imagined she might almost have pain with it. The full cheeks gave her face a robust, hearty quality not unlike Laura's. Victoria herself was tall and thought of herself as somewhat taut in the face.

'You left that front door open again,

Mummy, for the world and his wife to walk in on you.'

'Sure I was only shaking the mat and who would be walking in on me?'

'You never know who's about these days. I might have been a prowler looking for antiques.'

'Quit your worrying.' There came a chuckle. 'I've an antique in that top cupboard for fly boys like that. Do you want tea or coffee?'

Father's shotgun, presumably. Old Foxy. Victoria glanced up at the long, horizontal box fixed just below the ceiling. The lock was missing.

'A stiff whisky would be more like the thing,' she said, wondering about Laura. Evidently she hadn't been here, for Mother would have said straight out. 'Tea, please. You've had the same jar of coffee for the last five years.'

'Dear, dear, such a thing to say about a body. John used to say coffee was only fit for the Americans, God rest his soul. Did you see the rhubarb on the way in? You'll have to take the last of it home with you, it's lovely stewed.'

The conversation continued at long-distance as Victoria crossed the room and then, up on her toes, teased open the flap of the gun cupboard. It held for her still the attraction of a place that was out of bounds . . . 'This is where Daddy keeps his gun and you mustn't ever touch Old Foxy . . .' They had not lost all their force, the imperatives of long ago.

The gun was gone.

She did not know, for a moment, whether the jolt that hit her was shock or merely surprise. If it wasn't here . . . then where? Guns and children – you surely had to know where they were?

'The gun is gone, Mother,' she said in the kitchen.

'What?'

'Daddy's gun. You must have put it somewhere else.'

'No, I don't think so.'

'Then someone must have taken it, Mummy,' Victoria insisted.

A maverick thought had slithered across the borderline between sense and fantasy: and she pictured Laura among the rushes of the bottom fields with Old Foxy in her hands. She blinked the image away.

'Ach, sure I'm stupid, didn't I make Jim take it that time he helped me with the building and he wouldn't take a penny. And you're not yourself the day, Vicky, you're the same as you were when you went in for them music examinations.'

'Those were the days. I've asked Jim to meet me here, Mummy.'

Hardly a flicker as her mother raked the ashes in the stove with a blackened toasting-fork. 'Well, he's very welcome. And where is Laura?'

'At this moment I have no idea. I thought she might be here because . . . for some reason she took it into her head to go and see Jim. Which means that she must have been past your door not two hours ago.'

'On her own?' Mother straightened, her chubby face red with blood. 'Bless us! Girls are more trouble than boys, there never was a truer word spoke. But what for?'

To deliver a mouthful of incontinence, Victoria thought, but didn't say. To declare hand on heart that she would never be a Mulholland.

'Such a carry on! But can the two of you

not talk through this awkwardness between you, Vicky?'

'I have tried, Mummy. Yes.'

She declined the opportunity to say yet again that the talking never went anywhere; that after it stopped the silence set in like cement until she was reaching for the headache tablets. Foolish to come here, she thought.

'Vicky, you'll have to make her see that there's just the two of you and you've only got each other.'

'That is not the case, Mummy, which is my whole point! We haven't only got each other – she'll have a family of her own in a few years, and I can have Jim and be near you.'

'Don't you worry about me, dear, for I'll be all right.'

'Even without Old Foxy?' The joke was small, but precious in the context. Victoria hurried on as her mother smiled. 'I'm just saying that this move isn't just for me, it's the best thing for all of us – it will make Laura and me more independent of one another, not less. And that's how it should be. I know in my heart that I'm right about this.'

A pat on the hand from her mother. 'Well. You could always think your way through things brave and well, like one of them lawyers, your daddy used to say. That'll be Jim now, I know his hand on the door.'

Jim Mulholland came through the back door somewhat diffidently, as if he didn't want to bother it by obliging it to widen unnecessarily. This was not easy, for he had the largeness of frame that rugby players require in their scrums.

'Come on in, Jim.'

'A wild evenin', Mrs Stirling. Pardon the feet. You can't hang them up, more's the pity.'

'Oh, get away with you. But we haven't had it too bad all the same.'

'Up to the present, not too bad at all.'

Hearing these exchanges – savouring them, even, for they had a quality that spoke to her of the significance of place – and observing the enormity of his wrapped-up country presence in the small kitchen, Victoria found herself smiling at the thought of him wearing a gold medallion round his neck by a swimming pool in

Majorca. Did he hanker after steel guitars and Mediterranean moons and wine? Why not? But she, seeing him from boots to cap, frankly thought of the pleasure of earthing-up a drill of potatoes.

'It's nice to see you, Vicky.'

'And you, Jim.'

'Well, there's tea in the pot, Jim, so you can help yourself,' said Mother.

'I'm all right thanks, Mrs Stirling.'

'Fair enough. I'm away to find something to do.'

Victoria took him by the hands. 'These things are freezing.'

'Try holding my feet,' he said.

'Jim, just try holding me for a while. Peggy's pestering me to go to the Algarve with her. I could spend a week ensconced in this hug.'

'And it's a cheaper form of ensconcing.'

'Miser.'

'Practical. You know me, Vicky.'

Bob had always called her Victoria. Odd, that Jim should be one of a tiny band who shortened her name to Vicky. Perhaps the fact that she'd known him always made him acceptable to her now, she thought, because whatever good feeling he had for her had its basis in time. He brought to their relationship a retrospective recognition that she had once been more fit, more fresh, more frivolous, more ready for the opportunity and the risk. He'd known her at her best. Everybody's life, she surmised, has a cast of original players, and Jim Mulholland belonged to her in this way.

He set her to one side, stiffly, like a removal man with a tallboy. 'She was the spit of you, Vicky, standing in that barn.'

'Laura?'

'As you were, twenty years ago.'

'Really. I've never been struck by the resemblance, myself.'

Fate, Destiny, some Grand Old Force working them round in circles? Pure blind chance, she wanted to tell him: I became a widow, you never went to enough church socials to find the right girl and we're both available; that's all there is to it.

'Were you and Laura talking for a long time, or . . . ?'

'Not long, really, she didn't stay. There was no need for you to fly down here.'

'How could I just sit! I was sure she'd be

130

here. I can't get over it.'

'She was upset all right, mind you,' he conceded in a measured way. 'Looking back on it, I did the worst thing. It never helps any situation when you lose the head.'

'Huh. Join the club.'

'I should have tried to explain – let her see that I've got a point of view, at least. Should I ring her up, do you think?'

A glutton for punishment, she thought. 'No, you wouldn't get the better of her, Jim, even Mother blames me.'

'But how can she?'

To answer, she found, was too laborious. A child is one's life's work, the outstanding artefact . . . house and home and family, you can't aspire to anything higher . . . Maybe Mother is even right in her way, and I'm the odd-ball.

'What else did Laura say to you?'

'I told you most of it on the phone. Not a lot more, really, it was all in the way she conducted herself. Even the dog sensed it, I'm sure he did.'

'Sheer bad manners.'

'All the same, I'd say she was beyond caring about manners, to be fair. She said you were too old to have children without . . . well, without them being handicapped was what she meant, I suppose.'

Victoria's first thought was almost to smile. At least this dredging-up of some half-digested article in a magazine implied a peek into the future. But then the downright perversity of it angered her, made her see the remark as a wizening curse. Thou shalt bring forth a changeling!

'Why is she like this! Everything that's precious to her seems to be bound up in that ordinary little house, it's so basic, so . . . *territorial*. She's like an animal pacing up and down its boundaries ready to fly at anything that moves! I'm worried about her school work, Jim. She doesn't do a thing for school. What am I doing to her?'

His fingers, which had been mechanically drumming on the arms of a chair, came together under his jaw in the shape of a church steeple. An uncharacteristic gesture, accompanied by a gathering of the brows.

'She said she wasn't there to change my mind. That, and one or two other things she said made me think she might be getting ready to accept the situation. Grin and bear it, sort of thing.'

'She might bear it, but she'll never grin. She might hate you for ever, Jim.'

The steeples fell into his lap as he shrugged. 'That's the risk I'll have to take, then.'

But can I, she thought, as Mother came clattering in with a shovel of coal.

Thirteen

Mother and daughter passed one another on the very top step, just where the stairs flattened out in a royal blue sward of best quality Axminster, Victoria going up, Laura coming down. The former was on her way to check her appearance in the long bedroom mirror, the latter, to watch nothing special on television. It was one of those moments when bodies are closer together than they would normally be. Not to speak, to glide on by regardless after meeting headlong within the funnel of the stairs would not only have flouted the conventions of their particular war (and Rules of Engagement had evolved, even if they had never been articulated); it would also, more seriously, have downgraded the other person to the status of the stranger one may or may not greet on the moving escalator in Anderson and McAuley's. Each knew that the other would speak.

But the moment was fraught with

danger. For different reasons, neither had yet mentioned the events of yesterday – Laura because she could not be sure that her mother knew of her visit; Victoria because she had now made a decision, and talking about what had happened would not help. The least said now, soonest mended.

'Laura, would you by any chance know where I could lay my hands on a stamp?'

'I never use them. Try the drawer.'

'Oh, drawers, whoever thought them up should be shot. They're useless unless the only thing in them is what you're looking for.'

'You could try rummaging,' Laura said, 'like everybody else.'

And there the conversation might have ended, with due acknowledgements all round, had Laura not commented on her mother's appearance. Longish dress, dark green and mauve. Lustrous looking. High heels and lips reddened, probably for him.

'Where are you going all dressed up?'

'Out.'

'With Peggy?' she persisted. 'Or somebody else?'

'In a group. A Scottish company is giving

Il Trovatore at the Opera House and one must maintain one's interests in spite of everything. Anyway, it was booked months ago. And look at the time!'

Laura followed her up the landing. 'Is it OK if I ask somebody over?'

'Within reason. I don't think I'm ready for Bucket McKenzie just yet.'

'You don't know him, Mother.'

'The sound of him is enough.'

'So he hasn't got a musical name,' Laura said with a masking quietness, for she was thinking: more surgery! Now I'm to cut out Bucket McKenzie. 'You're not in a position to know the first thing about Bucket McKenzie and he might be one of the most intelligent people in the form for all you know. How would you like me to insult one of your friends like that?'

'Laura, do what you like, I'm past giving a damn. I have to go. According to Peggy there is a special place in Dante's *Inferno* for those who miss overtures.'

By now Victoria was inside her bedroom and circumnavigating the snags of the old worn linen-basket when the taunt reached her.

'There can't be many farmers who like opera. He must be one in a million.'

Laura did not hear the odd little gasp her mother gave, or see the convulsive movement with which she heaved the wounded spectre of herself away from the long mirror. She, Laura, was aware only of a presence at the top of the stairs which compelled her to turn round and look up. There loomed her mother, as still as the lathe-turned newel on which her left hand rested.

'What did you say?'

'When?'

'What did you say to me just now?'

After a pause, Laura said, 'I can't remember. How am I supposed to remember every single word I say?'

Again the question, more loudly, drilled down the stairs at her, shattering the lie. 'What did you say to me just now! Repeat it!'

'I said . . . Not many farmers like opera.'

Not the whole truth, but wholly a confession. Laura, utterly shaken, waited below the level of her mother's feet to be crushed.

'I'm only glad that your father cannot see what a hard and very, very ignorant little girl you have become, Laura.'

Her mother then passed her on the stairs, gathered up her coat and left the house.

In her mother's closing of the front door Laura expected to feel again, like a clash of cymbals, some of the grim rage which had been vibrating in that voice some moments before; but it didn't happen. There was no excess of energy, no slam, just the quiet habitual click, leaving Laura leaning on the banister, neither up nor down in the empty house.

It felt more than empty; it felt hollow, like herself, gutted of all happiness – it frightened her to think that not an echo remained of the laughter there must have been. Hard and ignorant.

She would have to go now, wouldn't she? This phenomenon had finally come to an end as things come to an end in the natural world, like monsoons, and hurricanes, and drought. Laura sat down on the third step up, thought of phoning Stephen who cherished her, then finally tapped

Julie's number instead without knowing why.

It was, she thought, like giving an account of a dream. Her voice sang out with a quality of theatrical good cheer. '. . . And that was more or less that, Julie. After calling me hard and ignorant away she went – flounced out of the house to see *Il Trovatore*.'

'And who's he when he's at home?'

'It's an opera, Julie. What does "ignorant" actually mean?'

'Witless. To be without gumption, to be brain dead after the fashion of Bucket McKenzie and you definitely don't qualify, Laura, because how many farmers round the country get huddled up to their hi-fis after milking the cows and pigs and listen to big fat foreign people singing? Let's face it – would you need a calculator?'

One could only smile, she thought. 'You'd better come and stay with me every weekend or I'll never speak to you again.'

'Stephen says you could buy a horse.'

'What for?'

'They've got four legs and you ride them, swivel-head. He's got a thing about dogs and horses, thinks they're therapeutic. And if you do get one, for God's sake don't make a mistake and saddle up a pig. I must go. We're visiting Aunt Belle's, she's the one with the false teeth who sucks barley sugar.'

'What am I going to do, Julie?'

'Well, what do I know? You could invite over the Bucket McKenzie connection for a barbeque in the back garden and let them cook the goldfish. That would let your mother know what hard and ignorant really means. On the other hand nobody's free, right? Make her a cup of tea when she comes in, Laura. You were never going to win, so as Lady Macbeth once said, when you know you're beat, lose with a bit of style. See you tomorrow.'

'Bye.'

Now she walked into the kitchen and saw the letter still propped against the radio where her mother had abandoned it. The name of Jim Mulholland was the first line in the neatly typed address. It had no stamp, and the flap was not stuck down or even tucked in. Laura washed her hands and dried them before carefully teasing out the letter to preserve the original folds.

For they were steaming open her life, weren't they, the two of them – smashing all her friendships into meaningless pulp, carting her off like an awkward piece of furniture that mightn't quite fit in where it was going, but which couldn't be left behind. She might not like what they were saying about her, but her right to know was as great as their right to privacy; and even if it wasn't, hard and ignorant for this last time she would be.

Unlike the address, the letter itself was handwritten.

Dear Jim,

What you said on the phone is true, but there's more than one truth, don't you see? When it comes down to it how can I be sure that at her age she'll put down roots again, and not wither, one wouldn't do it to a tree. She may need this place, Jim. She may not cling to me personally, but I can only think that she needs to be here for a little longer. Perhaps in the end things have made me deeply pessimistic about life, I'm just not brave enough to make

another start. Maybe I'm just exhausted.
Anyway, there it is. I do have to add that
to me you are the salt of the earth. I use
the phrase because I never did appreciate
its meaning until I tasted you, Jim, but
no, my dear friend, I'm truly sorry.
    With deep affection,
    Vicky.

Laura replaced the letter and settled the
envelope against the radio at the proper
angle. Then she sat down at the table and
supported her face with the palms of her
hands as if, armed with this victory, now
she could let the tears flow for herself and
her mother, both. Nothing in the whole
wide world, she knew, could save her from
the next few minutes.

Scalding hot, the rivers ran down the
valleys of her face. They gathered at the
point of her chin, and dripped away. They
leaked in at the corners of her mouth and
tasted salty on her tongue, as the salt of the
earth is salty. The heaving and the sobbing
came in such squalls that she could only
hold on to the rim of the table and submit to
their convulsive force. From time to time

she stared wildly at the ceiling through blurred eyes, and gasped in air through her mouth, for her nose had filled with a thick mucus; and not a thought was in her head but that it was like this in the beginning, when you were born, only your tiny mind didn't know to remember.

When some minutes of this had passed she felt her body loosen. God, she thought, what a sight I must look.

Presently she looked for a number in the address book – hall chest, second drawer down – and made sure of the proper code in the telephone directory.

He's maybe at the opera, she thought, and what the devil am I going to say to him? Put a saddle on the pig?

Jim Mulholland answered.